# KINGDOM OF LOVE
## Hannah Hurnard

Tyndale House Publishers, Inc.
Wheaton, Illinois

Tenth printing, February 1983

Library of Congress Catalog Card Number 75-13945
ISBN 0-8423-2080-6, paper
United States publications rights secured by
Tyndale House Publishers, Inc., Wheaton, Illinois 60187.
Published with the permission of The Church's Ministry
Among the Jews (Olive Press), London, England.
American edition copyright © 1978 by
Tyndale House Publishers, Inc.
Reset and reissued, May 1979
Printed in the United States of America

# Contents

# Preface

How utterly and unspeakably dreary and dark is the realm of our thought life, and mind or heart of our being, when self reigns there and produces and directs the habits of thought which make us the individuals which we are. But when the whole realm of the mind and thought life passes out of the control of self altogether, and becomes the kingdom of our Lord and Savior, Holy Love himself, how complete and radiant is the transformation. It is like a new creation altogether. "There cometh one after me," cried John the Baptist exultantly, "who shall baptize you with the Holy Ghost and with fire," the fire of holy love.

For years I sadly supposed that such a glorious experience as the kingdom of love extending into and controlling the whole realm of my mind and thought life must be postponed until I should pass out of this earthly life into heaven. And then at last, I too discovered what the early Christians so rejoiced and exulted in (and a great multitude of the Lord's lovers in every generation since), the thing which made them so completely radiant and charged with life and power, namely that it is God's purpose to translate us into the kingdom of his dear Son, now here on earth, and that it is most gloriously possible to be, as it were, annexed to heaven, even before we leave the body.

We are to experience the reign of our Lord and Savior who is Holy Love, completely controlling our whole thought life, and converting our minds into realms of radiant, creative love. Love always, and only, thinks lovely thoughts, so that the minds in which the Lord of Love makes his kingdom become kingdoms of light instead of darkness, and enjoy a foretaste of the glory and joy of the creative life and work of heaven itself.

This little book seeks to share very simply with other self-wearied and longing Christians something of the glory of this discovery.

# CHAPTER 1
# Lost Love

"... I have one thing against thee, ... Thou hast left thy first love" (Rev. 2:4).

"My faith burns low, my hope burns low,
Only my heart's desire cries out in me,
By the deep thunder of its want and woe,
Cries out to Thee."

Christina Rossetti

In the courtyard of our house in Jerusalem there was an old rusty pump connected with an underground cistern stretching beneath the paved yard. In 1948, during the months when the Jewish half of Jerusalem was besieged by Arab armies, who controlled the pipe line and prevented any water from reaching the besieged area, that cistern, with its cranky, creaking pump, was an unspeakably precious possession. We knew that as long as water remained in the cistern, our needs would be met.

But what a pump it was! So aged, and stubborn and resistant, we were sometimes completely exhausted before we could raise enough water to fill even one pail. There was the cistern, deep and wide, and containing enough to meet all our needs and those of friends and neighbors as well, all through the long dry summer months until the rains would come again and refill it, but the daily labor involved in making the water available for use was tremendous.

Thousands of other people with no cistern of their own had to line up, often under heavy shell fire, to wait for their daily water carts distributing the ration allowed by the municipality, and after that, those who lived in high buildings had to carry or haul up to the top floor every drop of the precious fluid, fearing all the time that some might spill over and be lost. But rich as our supply of water made us in comparison with others, the ancient, long used pump which raised it to the surface was a most exhausting connecting link between the supply and our need.

Five years later, after traveling more than halfway around the world, I stepped out of a motor coach, and walking a few steps towards a low parapet, I looked out on one of the most awe-inspiring sights I have ever seen—Niagara Falls.

I saw a great river flowing swiftly towards a vast cliff, and pouring itself over the lip of rock, to fall hundreds of feet in a thundering cascade. The spray rose in drenching clouds, higher than the cliffs themselves, and the thunder and roar of the falls filled the whole region. The power engendered by the river, as it poured itself from the heights above to the depths below, when harnessed by the power station at the foot of the falls, was great enough to provide electric current for some of the greatest cities in the world.

The first sight of that irresistible flood of water almost took one's breath away. The river flowed swiftly between green and wooded banks, till it came to the place of complete self-giving, to the great crisis in its course, where it must leap down to a lower place, giving itself in an ecstasy of abandonment and, in so doing, experience life and power more abundant.

By very force of contrast, the memory of the cranky old Jerusalem pump came vividly before me, as so often I had stood beside it, praying desperately, "O Lord, help me to make the water come and fill these buckets!" What a contrast! The pump trickle and the Niagara Falls!

I thought of the words of another weary woman in Palestine, long centuries ago, "Sir, thou hast nothing to draw with and the well is deep." And then as I looked at the mighty flow of water over Niagara Falls, my heart cried out exultantly, "The river of God is full of water." We have no need of pumps where his fullness is concerned.

It often seemed to me in Jerusalem that our ancient cranky pump, which, though it provided us with as much water as we were prepared to labor for, exhausted our strength and energy and never by any chance gushed forth spontaneously, displayed a certain disconcerting similarity to much of our missionary work and witness in the Holy Land. Since the time of the Crusades in the Middle Ages, the Holy Land remained subject to Moslem domination, until at last, in 1918, at the end of World War I, a Christian Mandatory Government took over the control of Palestine, after what has been called the last crusade under General Allenby.

It was only natural, when this great event happened, that almost every Christian nation in the world should desire to be represented in the land where the Christian church was born, and where the greatest events in the world's history took place. So that by the end of the Mandate, thirty years later, it was calculated that about eighty different Protestant missions, communities and denominations were at work in the Holy

City, Jerusalem. This, of course, does not include the very numerous branches of the Latin and Eastern churches working there also.

It can easily be seen, therefore, that this situation presented many difficulties and unfortunate complications. If, for example, a Jew or Moslem finally decided to follow the Lord Jesus openly, he had of necessity to choose which of these eighty or so foreign Protestant groups he would join, and then he was not really expected to have fellowship with the other seventy-nine groups, for fear he should be lured away to join some more "spiritual" or more "worldly" church, or be snared into joining some unscriptural cult or "ism," some "devil's counterfeit organization;" or possibly (looked at from a rather different angle) some "heretical group with no ordained ministry, and therefore not a church at all."

This situation, of course, most unhappily, is not unknown in some Christian lands, but it may be difficult to realize just what it involves in a non-Christian country. From the non-Christian onlooker's point of view, as he perhaps reads with curious interest the New Testament so earnestly pressed upon him by some member of one of these many Christian groups, it must seem that the prayer of the Christian's Lord and Savior, when he prayed that his followers might be one, had received a strange answer; that becoming a member of the Christian church, and knowing which other members of the Body to maintain fellowship with, and which were spurious growths, must be a most complicated and difficult affair.

Some of us (and I was certainly among the most zealous in this) also spent a good deal of time and energy in accusing others of pulling down and destroying what we sought to build up, and in diligently pointing out these unsound workmen and warning against them. But the honest, though rather extraordinary, truth is that we did in actual fact long for God's glory, and to be faithful in our service and witness to him.

Indeed it was our very zeal and longing that his command should be fulfilled and the gospel be preached to all people, which made us so prone to distrust others, so dogmatically sure of the exclusive rightness of our way and distinctive message. Others certainly were just as dogmatically sure that their teachings were true, each of us had the same conviction—we were right and they were wrong!

As Christians we knew, of course, the actual physical persecution of those who disagreed with us would be quite wrong and un-Christlike, but we had this in common with Saul of Tarsus, "we were exceedingly zealous of the traditions of"—the evangelicals—and we "verily thought that we ought to do many things," to thwart the witness of those who differed from us in doctrine, belief and practice, and who we feared would lead young converts—babes in Christ—into deplorable and dangerous errors.

Our Lord knows that that is what we feared and dreaded, always the fear for our babes in Christ and the young converts. But we only knew the old, old method, practiced with such disastrous results down through the ages, the method of destructive criticism, under the guise of warning others. Strangely enough we seemed so pathetically ineffective in grounding these precious babes and young converts in the life of utter surrender to Christ himself, where, rooted and grounded in him, they would remain absolutely unresponsive to any teaching which would dim their love and personal devotion to him.

So we went on, praying earnestly for revival, that God would sweep away all that was only nominal Christianity, and burn and consume with holy fire all that was false and spurious.

Then something happened. The British Mandate ended in 1948, and as war between the Arabs and Jews was seen to be inevitable once the British forces withdrew, all foreigners in Palestine were warned and urged to leave the country, until more peaceful conditions should return. Most of them did leave, and, in the course of a few months, practically every Protestant institution in the Jewish half of Palestine closed down; the different Christian congregations were scattered far and wide, and the majority of missionaries withdrew (it was hoped only temporarily) from the country.

About twelve foreign missionaries, how-ever, were permitted by the Jews to remain in the Jewish half of Jerusalem when Parti-tion took place in May 1948, and they thus shared with a hundred thousand Jews the months of siege, during which the Arab armies of Egypt and Transjordan surround-ed Jewish Jerusalem, completely isolating it for nearly a year from the rest of the State of Israel. I have written about those experiences during the months of siege, in *Watchmen on the Walls*, and of the intense earnest longing which then filled our hearts, that spiritual revival should at last break out in Jerusalem, and that a united Christian witness be the outcome.

A fire had indeed swept over the Holy Land, the storm of war had scattered the Christian communities far and wide, and surely a new era was now to begin, and from rock bottom, as it were, was to be built up in the power of the Holy Spirit, a united church and witness to Israel. So, as soon as the siege drew to a close, and it was safe to walk abroad in the streets, realizing how few we were and how great our need to unite together in fellowship and worship, we began meeting together, once a week, in each other's mis-sion houses, to pray for revival and for en-duement with power, that, like the early Christians, we might be able to give together a Christian witness in the Holy City—"with power and with signs following."

Happily, in spite of diversity of opinions, we were all sufficiently in earnest to continue attending the prayer meetings, but it became more and more painfully evident that the ideal of "All of one mind, in one place," was not going to be easy to achieve.

There was, too, the problem of our "united" evangelistic witness to the people of Israel. Some of the group felt strongly that from then on the missions should all unite in their public witness to the Jews and non-Christians, regardless of the different denominations which the missions represented, and that once a week, at least, a united service should be held (instead of all the different denominational ones), to which the public should be invited. But once again the immense diversity of our languages, our differing needs and temperaments, intellectual differences and requirements became very obvious.

What form of service should this united witness follow? All the ministers, with their differing ideas as to how a service should be conducted, would have to lead the meeting in turn. It must be evangelistic, because its aim was to reach non-Christian people. But here a difficulty arose—it could not possibly take the place of our services for worship on Sunday.

Very well, let it be held at some other hour, either on Sunday, the Christian day of worship, or, better still, on Saturday, the Jewish day of worship, when most of the non-Christians could attend if they wished to do so. All of them, of course, had to work on the Christian's Sunday. Let the different ministers, in turn, conduct this evangelistic meeting just as they felt led, and it would give us all the opportunity of learning to adapt ourselves to ways which other groups had found helpful, but which were unfamiliar to us. In this way, by being willing to sink our differences on some occasions, we could all be helped, and prove the Lord's willingness to use and bless a variety of methods.

In theory this sounded perfect, but in practice it never materialized. There seemed to be no hour during the week when everybody could be free at the same time. Without exception, all these zealous and devoted missionaries were busy with their own meetings and classes, and though, if there had been real conviction that the united service was God's will, this difficulty could, no doubt, have been overcome, it transpired that not even half of us felt that such a weekly meeting was desirable.

People were willing enough to attend such a meeting when their own trusted minister was to lead, which would happen about once in three months, but many just did not feel inspired to go through eleven other meetings, carried on in a "dreary," or "depressing," or "formal," or "emotional" form, which by experience they had already found did not help them or the rest of their congre-

16

gation. But most difficult of all was the fact that our method and way of presenting the Christian message differed so greatly. And, moreover, the points we felt consciously obliged to emphasize were so divergent.

It was feared that though a man might preach only the gospel at those united meetings, if he proved to be a very inspiring speaker, members of other congregations might be lured to listen to him in his own church, and so come under the influence of his "unsound interpretation" of other parts of the Scriptures. It was the old distrust and fear. Young converts and babes in Christ must not be endangered before they were sufficiently developed to know how to choose the good and to reject error. So that our personal reactions to the idea of a weekly united service of witness were expressed even more strongly than those concerning the weekly prayer meeting.

In the end, the idea of a weekly united witness, at which all the churches would be present, was decided to be an unnecessary and impracticable scheme. It was felt that every denomination had its own special contribution to make, in its own way. We had all been called of God to witness to Israel, and we should surely do well to concentrate on witnessing to the groups with which we were already in contact. We were so diverse in temperament and need, that all the different and distinctive forms of worship seemed needed if all were to be suited and helped.

But we decided that we would encourage the members of our congregations who were able to be free on Tuesday afternoons, to attend the united prayer meetings, thus gaining a true understanding of the fact that though we differ in so many ways, and cannot all get help from the same forms, that we are indeed all one in Christ Jesus. In love and devotion to him we can feel ourselves united to one another also, even though we find we are so made that we need to express that love, devotion and obedience in many differing ways and forms.

And every Christmas and Easter we would all unite in a great public meeting in the Y.M.C.A. auditorium, with the ministers of all the churches on the platform, with their congregations uniting together to sing the Christmas and Easter hymns, showing to our non-Christian neighbors, who always seemed ready to come to a service of good music, that we really could unite in expressing love and thanksgiving to our Lord, who for love's sake had become a man, and then for love of the whole world had died upon the cross. This seemed to us as far as we were able to go.

To one person at least these developments came as a devastating, almost agonizing shock. And that person was myself. Brought up and trained as I had been in a strictly fundamentalist environment, I had never doubted during my first years on the mission field that we were absolutely right in emphasizing the vital importance of sound doctrine and complete separation from the world, and that where others differed from us in their interpretation of what was sound doctrine and what constituted worldliness, they were wrong.

On the other hand, for a long time I had not been able to accept the extreme position of those who maintained that those who differed from us were all too likely not born-again Christians at all. My attitude was that they just hadn't got the fuller light that we evangelicals had, and consequently were more worldly, and less interested in evangelistic work. Vital as I considered doctrine to be, I thought that quarrels about differences in forms of worship and outward expression of our devotion to God were quite unimportant, and that everybody ought to be free to follow their own conscience in such matters.

What a man believed in the way of doctrine was important, because it would affect his whole conduct and understanding of spiritual things; but his ideas about external observances seemed to me (with my Quaker upbringing) comparatively unimportant, and certainly not worthwhile arguing about. I had taken for granted that when all nominal Christians, Modernists and worldly Christians were removed from the mission field, and only sincere devoted evangelicals remained, the Keswick ideal of "All one in Christ Jesus" would automatically follow, and we would find true unity at last.

And now, here we were, a small group of Christian missionaries, left alone in Jewish Jerusalem, all evangelicals; all devoted enough to have left home and country in order to obey our Lord's command to preach the gospel to every creature. Yet we were no more united by our fundamental doctrines, and our evangelical outlook, and apparently, no more endued with power from on high, than we had been during the years when we had been prone to put the blame for the ineffectiveness and weakness of missionary work in Palestine on to the leavening influence of so many non-evangelical groups in our midst!

For the first time I began to realize that the secret of real unity and power does not lie in the realm of doctrine at all. I was face to face, at last, with the fact that fundamental doctrines and the label "evangelical" have no real power to unite the Lord's people. Apparently, too, it is not enough to achieve united prayer meetings where the Lord's people ask for this unity and power. Neither is a sincere wish and longing in the hearts of his people for unity and power sufficient to produce it, nor self-sacrifice for the sake of the work. All the things which I had unhesitatingly believed were the means by which this unity and power would come were proving a failure, and I was forced at last to face the fact that the secret of unity and power must lie somewhere else.

It became the almost agonized longing and desire of my heart to find the secret. If unity of desire to witness for the Lord, to preach the gospel to every creature, and to obey the Lord as far as we had the light, would not really unite us, could not make us trust one another, least of all, could not, in many cases, enable us even to like one another and to be willing to cooperate together—then what could? What secret did the early Christians have, which we apparently had lost?

During the months when we were making this devastating discovery in Jerusalem, I went to spend a brief holiday in Cyprus, determined to lay aside everything else, and to face this matter with the Lord. I stayed in a little village high up on Mount Olympus. And there I made daily walks in different directions around the mountain. From Olympus there were wonderful, far-reaching views across intervening valleys and plains, to another chain of glorious mountain peaks on the opposite side of the island.

One day as I followed a new path along the mountainside, I was struck by the totally new aspects and appearance of that distant range of mountains, as I saw it from different points of view along the winding pathway. In fact, from some points on Mount Olympus, I could scarcely believe that I was looking at the very same peaks which I saw every day from the village in which I was staying. The scene which I looked at most often was the most familiar, and, as it happened, the most beautiful of all the views, but it was not the whole scene, and it did not reveal more than a small part of the whole mountain range. I could not possibly tell someone staying in another village, on a different part of Mount Olympus, that the view they described was false because it differed from what I was able to see from my own limited viewpoint.

All I could do was to walk to their village, look at their view, and congratulate myself that, on the whole, the village in which I had the good fortune to find myself had a finer and more extensive view than theirs. But none of the villages on Mount Olympus, grand and far reaching as their views generally were, could see more than a fraction of the reality and extent and richness of that great, far-reaching range opposite us. And there were many things we could not see clearly because we were too far from them and distance distorted them.

It occurred to me with great comfort and relief that our different doctrinal interpretations are only parts of the whole truth, differing because of necessity, due to environment, teaching, temperament and intellectual variations, and because we are looking at truth from different angles. Most of us look only at the familiar and accustomed views which we have come to love and venerate, just because they belong to our environment and seem so naturally and beautifully right, forgetting that, even so, they are not the whole truth.

Some Christians have, as it were, special and favorite paths which they always follow, and which lead them to certain viewpoints which particularly fascinate them, although quite admittedly they open out on only a narrow and particular point on the whole mountain range of truth. For example, some people have become enamored of a certain path, which always ends in the prophet Daniel, looking at the "great image" or "the Beast" or, perhaps, "the Army of the North." Others go straight and always to the opening chapters of the Acts of the Apostles or to the gifts of the Spirit in 1 Cor. 12, as though the heart and fullness of the whole truth centered just there.

Some people always follow the particular thought path which brings them to their favorite view place, and regard with deep distrust any suggestion that they might take a look at the range of truth from quite a different angle. Worse than that, things which are invisible from their own viewpoint they denounce as untrue, as heresies, whereas if they would only dare to venture a little further on and look honestly from a rather different angle, they might conceivably see that these heretical and perhaps distorted ideas are really part of another glimpse of the full truth. It is truth, and not our partial understanding of it, which saves.

Our doctrines, and even the things the

church has always taught, are only men's interpretations of what is written in the Bible. The things which are written there are true; they are either accounts of what eye-witnesses actually saw and heard, or what they wrote under the guidance of the Holy Spirit. The doctrines as we understand them are the interpretations of sincere Christians; and it is a fact of history that the greatest saints in all the different ages have varied in their interpretations of what is written in the Bible. Sound doctrine (or teaching, as it is in the Greek) is what is written in the Bible. And alas, so often what we mean by funda-mental doctrines is a particular tradition or school of interpretation; in other words the traditions of men.

But even the Bible, rich and full as it is of truth from beginning to end, cannot be properly understood except in the light of one's personal experience of Christ himself. He is the truth, the full truth. Only as we follow him in obedience can we come to know more and more of truth. The whole Bible points us to him as the way, the truth and the life; and there in the heart of the gospel itself we hear the voice of God speak-ing and saying, "This is my beloved Son—hear him."

The realization which came to me there on Mount Olympus, with the overwhelming power and joy of an entirely new conception, has been beautifully summed up by a Chris-tian writer, who said, "Christian unity is not possible unless delegates agree not to press their doctrinal difference. . . . . The way to unity of doctrine is not by definitions, but by practicing the unity of the Spirit, in the bonds of love, on the way to knowing the full truth, concerning Jesus. And the way to know him is not by argument and speculation, but by obeying him and walking with him. If any man will do his will, he shall know of the doctrine."

How strange it is, too, that we should be so desperately afraid that God will allow the most earnest and seeking souls to be deluded, if in their longing search for his truth, they begin to explore other thought paths, or wish to try for themselves some path which other earnest Christians have found to be helpful. It is true those other ways may not prove helpful to all, and in that case we may surely wait restfully in the certainty that, if some special brand of Christian experience which does not appeal to us personally is not going to help our friends either, God will bring them to see this, after they have honestly tested it for themselves. We have in this connection the very words and promise of our Lord himself.

"What man is there of you, who, if his son ask bread, will he give him a stone? Or if he ask fish, will he give him a serpent. If ye then, being evil, know how to give good gifts unto your children, how much more shall your Father which is in heaven give good things to them that ask him."

I returned to Jerusalem full of this new delivering and liberating realization, but still conscious that the whole problem had not been solved. Far from it. For the worst part still remained. What was the secret of real unity and power? If it lay in bringing every Christian to accept the fact that they must not press their doctrinal differences and different methods of worship, we were no better off than before, and no nearer a solution.

For there seemed absolutely no way of changing one another's points of view and personal convictions. For we all held these opinions conscientiously, believing they were the only true interpretations of the Scriptures, and like our forefathers before us, to a man and a woman we felt that we ought to be prepared, if necessary (and by the grace of God), to go to the stake rather than give them up.

But there we were, pumping and pumping for unity and power to witness to the unsaved, Christ-rejecting peoples around us, and nothing but a pitiful trickle came in response to all our effort. We sincerely longed for God's highest and best, but we seemed to find no way to achieve it.

Wherein did the secret lie? That was the burning question. Where was Niagara? And what actually did it mean to be baptized with the Holy Ghost and with fire? What was the great lack in our lives? What did the early Christians possess which we apparently had lost?

But above all, by this time, the question in my own heart seemed to have crystallized down to this: How can I personally experience a real love for, and unity with, other sincere Christians who have points of view I utterly disagree with and shrink from, and whose personalities, alas, I actively dislike?

I now say that I must cease to judge (pass sentence on) their various and, to me, most peculiar and unattractive ideas. But how can I really love them? And how far should I seek to cooperate with them?

Over and over again in my heart, at that time, I seemed to hear the Lord saying, to me most of all, and with increasing challenge and solemnity, "You have left your first love" (Rev. 2:4).

More and more as I pondered on the context of those words I came to feel that the church in Jerusalem today has much in common with the church of Ephesus of long ago. Both so zealous in exactly the same way, for the list of good things mentioned by the Lord is exactly what we set most store by in our missionary work. And yet apparently, without realizing it, both suffering from a terrible and vital lack, which threatened even to extinguish our lamp of witness altogether. "These things saith he that holdeth the seven stars in his right hand, and walketh in the midst of the seven candlesticks.

"I know thy works, and thy labor, and thy patience, and how thou canst not bear them which are evil, and how thou hast tried them which say they are prophets and are not, and hast found them liars. And hast borne, and hast patience, and for my name's sake has labored and hast not fainted.

"Nevertheless, I have somewhat against thee, because thou hast left thy first love. Remember therefore from whence thou art fallen, and do the first works, or else I will come unto thee quickly, and will remove thy candlestick out of his place, except thou repent" (Rev. 2:1-5).

# CHAPTER 2
# Kingdom of Love

"And when he was demanded of the Pharisees when the kingdom of God should come, he answered them and said . . ..'Behold the kingdom of God is within you' " (Luke 17: 20, 21).

As a man thinketh in his heart—so is he" (Prov. 23:7).

I had two special friends who had been with me through all the deep heart-searching and challenging experiences of the siege.

And in this ever-increasing longing and search for the secret of power and unity we three, at least, were absolutely one. This longing was like an unquenchable thirst, and we met together every week to pray that it might be satisfied. But even in that case also we were not exactly agreed as to what it was for which we were praying. We did know that we wanted to be baptized with the Holy Ghost and with fire, in the way that the Lord had promised, in order that we might be endued with power from on high, so that we might be able to bear witness to our Lord in a way that would challenge and convince the non-Christians around us.

We didn't seek this power just for ourselves, but longed that it might be the experience of the whole church in Jerusalem. We were coming to perceive more and more surely that we needed something new to happen in our own lives, first of all. It was not simply that we differed in points of doctrine and interpretation of parts of the Scriptures, but we were forced to recognize that there was something wrong, somewhere deep down in ourselves, deeper than the purely intellectual plane, where we could not see eye to eye. Perhaps deep, deep down, hidden away out of sight, it might even be that we did not want to see eye to eye, because we did not like one another, or resented certain things in one another.

Perhaps even stronger than our criticisms of one another's ideas was a far deeper criticism of another's faults and weaknesses and exasperating temperamental uncongenialities. Perhaps, even, we were jealous, or oversensitive, ambitious for spiritual preeminence or for leadership, determined to have our own way, unready to forgive, hotly impatient with the blemishes of others. Instead of being like the early Christians, were we not in actual fact, much more like the Pharisees of old, condemning others and feeling superior ourselves?

As I have said before, we three longed and prayed for the same experience of baptism with the Holy Spirit, but we were not in full agreement as to how it was to happen.

"Valiant" believed that if we were baptized with the Spirit we would begin to witness with irresistible power, with signs following, miracles of healing, speaking with tongues, etc., and that multitudes would be swept into the kingdom. The church of Christ would then inspire such holy awe and dread that no imposters or mere "hangers on" would dare join themselves with us, and so we would all worship together, with all the different forms swept away forever.

In the same way all our different interpretations would be swept away too, and we should be led into all truth, believing exactly the same things with no variations at all, because truth is one exact standard with no room for any variations. "Valiant" believed that we would receive this glorious experience when we all sought it together, tarrying

31

for it, all of one mind in one place.

"Loving Kindness," on the other hand, hoped and believed that the great characteristic of such a baptism would be that all barriers of every kind among the Lord's people would be swept away completely—denominational barriers, doctrinal differences and especially mission rivalries. We would all concentrate on building up the one Church of Christ and not our own individual missions. Most of all, the barriers between Hebrew and Gentile Christians would be broken down, the Gentiles humbling themselves to give an equal place to the Hebrews, and the Hebrews willing to appreciate Gentiles also. We would all be on fire for the Lord, and an absolutely united witness be given.

As for myself, looking despairingly into my own heart, as I had been forced to do through the entirely new and searching experiences of the siege, and realizing my own deepest need, I hoped and prayed that baptism with the Holy Spirit would mean baptism with holy love—nothing but love, a fire of love which would weld us together into one. I looked and longed for the welding flame of holy love, but I knew that I did not really know what holy love was, nor what it would mean if I suddenly found myself immersed in what I had so often sung about, "pure calvary love, which wins the lost to Thee."

All I knew was that all my life long my heart seemed to have been empty of true love toward others. I was sure that I loved my Lord himself; but then there was that almost terrible verse in 1 John 4:20, which asks, "he that loveth not his brother whom he hath seen, how can he love God whom he hath not seen?" I had been a missionary for nearly twenty years, and had lived and worked with really devoted fellow missionaries. And once again I must honestly bear witness to the fact that in my experience, the evangelical doctrines, if believed in sincerely, and if their implications be honestly accepted and followed, do produce an outstandingly earnest, untiring and splendidly devoted type of missionary, willing to go all lengths in sacrifice and suffering, in a supreme effort to win souls.

But I must also confess that this is not always the case. Through some inner distortion, or overemphasis of some doctrines at the expense of others, or allowing them to remain only theoretical formulas in the intellect and not life forces, a completely different type can be, and has been, developed, producing some of the hardest, most dogmatic and difficult-to-live-with Christians that it is possible to meet, or, at the other extreme, those who are so heavenly-minded that they are no earthly use.

The doctrine of salvation by grace alone and not of works, if it becomes unbalanced, or isolated from the rest of the truth, can leave a person as self-indulgent, unconscientious about work, lazy, uncooperative, tactless, and above all, critical of others, as it is possible to be. In my own case I knew with the most bitter and distressed realization that, despite sincere devotion to the evangelical doctrines for over twenty years, I was still able to remain absolutely lacking in true love towards many of my own fellow-workers, and in fact, towards the human race in general.

No doubt there were causes (as the modern psychologists would explain), dating back to my early childhood, which would account in large measure for the fact that I never felt spontaneous love for others. Until I was nineteen (as I have told in *The Hearing Heart*) I felt completely separated from other people, by reason of a very distressing stammer, and extreme oversensitiveness and morbid exaggeration of this handicap had caused me to dislike other people very much indeed, and to shun their company completely.

But I also realize that in my case the doctrine of original sin and the total depravity of the human nature, in which I had been brought up, had been subconsciously distorted in my mind to confirm me in the feeling and conviction, which my handicap of a stammer fostered, that all human beings were indeed very unpleasant creatures, with nothing naturally likeable about them, full of faults and blemishes, as well as being capable of the most horrible sins and corruptions; that though God

34

himself chose (for some mysterious reason) to love them, there was really nothing lovable about them, and that the Bible endorsed my own personal feeling that they were very unlikeable indeed, and most of them would, justly, be outcast and condemned for ever.

If there is any excuse at all, why I, of all people, should be writing this book, it lies just here, that as far as experience of even natural human love goes, I have started at rock bottom, that is, with none at all. And it may be that those unhappy people who by temperament and infirmity seem to have been born without a natural capacity to love, and who, by the grace of God, have been brought to learn it step by step, may be able to describe the manner in which they learned to love more clearly, perhaps, than some who have always loved spontaneously and normally.

During my whole childhood I never remember feeling love for anyone, not even my parents. Until I was nearly twenty I never remember liking anybody at first sight, though some seemed less obviously unlikeable than others. And though at my conversion the overwhelming glory and wonder of the love of Christ himself, the King of Love, broke into my wretched, cold little heart with amazingly transforming power, and for the first time I felt what it was to love him, yet it seemed to me that I never would learn to love other human beings spontaneously and with joy.

I did learn to love some of them very much indeed, but it was always a very slow business, and only after much struggle and real self-humiliation, and generally pain. All through my missionary life, as I gradually came to understand more fully what it was I lacked so terribly, and saw the Lord's love as the standard set before us, the one prayer that I prayed above all others was that I might learn to love—to feel love for those I worked with, and to like people naturally and spontaneously, instead of always seeing their faults and weaknesses so quickly and clearly, and missing all their nice characteristics.

It may be thought strange indeed that with this terrible difficulty over loving others I should become a missionary. Doesn't the missionary go abroad just because he feels love and compassion for the heathen and longs to bring to them the knowledge of Christ? One of the fundamental doctrines in which I had been brought up was that those who never heard the gospel of our Lord Jesus would be lost eternally, and that more than a million of them were dying every minute without having heard. Therefore all who were free and able to do so would certainly be constrained by the love of Christ to go and preach the gospel to them, and to rescue these perishing souls from eternal destruction.

But when I went as a missionary I was

under no illusion at all about my motive. As far as I was concerned it was not love of the heathen and desire to rescue them from hell which constrained me to be a missionary. Far from it. I believed the doctrine, and it did awaken pity and compassion in my heart, but in actual fact, accepting the doctrine did not produce the power to love and feel compassion for them in anything like a strong enough degree to make such a shrinking, terrified nature as mine willing to face life on the mission field. No.

All I knew was that the Lord Jesus had come to me, and made himself known to me in overwhelming love and glory, and that all my heart went out to him, and I must follow hard after him. He loved these countless millions whom he had made, and for some extraordinary reason he wanted me, who didn't feel any love for them at all, to go and tell as many as possible about his love for them. It was when I obeyed and went forth in this way and began telling others about him, that for the first time in my life I began to feel real love for others.

As I went up and down in the villages of England, and then from house to house in Palestine, speaking of the Lord Jesus and how he transforms life, I have known what it is to love. Sometimes while standing on the doorstep of a house, while perhaps somebody spat and cursed the name of our Lord and reviled me, I have felt an almost overmastering love and compassion and desire to help, and have known it was no love of my own cold heart, but something temporarily flooding through me from the source of love himself.

I have sat on vermin infested mats and mattresses in indescribably filthy mud huts, while the gospel was preached to men and women whose whole appearance and close proximity seemed an almost unbearable offense to my natural feelings, and have felt over and over again that other love from outside myself welling up in my heart and flooding out towards them. And whenever I preach or speak about him I know that love, the joy and ecstasy of it, and an immense compassion. But how I have known the lack of it at other times. Why? That was the question I asked myself over and over again in Jerusalem, after years on the mission field, and especially whenever we three friends were praying to be baptized with the Holy Spirit.

Why should I feel the Lord's love only when preaching and visiting from house to house, and why feel so different back on the mission compound, and in my daily contacts with other Christians why be so hard, so critical, so quick to see faults and so impatient with them? So unable, generally, to feel the same compassionate sympathy and love towards fellow Christians and non-Christians with whom I had ordinary everyday contacts? Why was I still so incapable of loving all the time? Why, if it was my Lord's own love which filled my heart sometimes, did it not fill my heart always?

And so week by week, as we prayed for revival, and day by day in my own prayer times, my prayer always was, "Lord, baptize me with holy love. I do not pray any longer to feel natural love. I pray to be baptized into thyself, thou who art love—that I may be set down in love, and be filled with love, and be kept in love the whole time." I longed with an ever intensifying, almost desperate desire to escape from the rusty pump experience of trying to force love in my daily life, and to be swept into the Niagara experience of utter surrender to his love the whole time.

Our blessed Lord himself has said, "Blessed are those that hunger and thirst . . . for they shall be filled." Perhaps someone is reading this who has thirsted for years to escape from the rusty pump experience of trying to force up love for those they have to live and work with, and to be swept away out into the Niagara flood of his mighty, never-ceasing love. It is blessed indeed to have such a thirst, for he means to satisfy it.

When at last I reached this stage of understanding that what I really meant when I prayed to be baptized and filled with the Holy Spirit was to be baptized into holy love, then the answer could be given. For I realize now that we pray for many things without really knowing what we are praying for. And while that is still the case, we are unready and unfit to receive them. And until we realize that what we really need is to have Love himself indwelling us, then we cannot receive him in all his fullness. The Spirit of him who raised Jesus from the dead is to dwell in us (Rom. 8:11).

Until this is understood it may be impossible for us to be baptized with the Holy Ghost because in our minds we confuse that with the thought of power to witness, or with the gift to work signs and wonders, or with the ability to speak with tongues, or with the power to heal the sick, or with great success in winning souls. Baptism means to be immersed in something—or someone, and that something or someone is Holy Love. Love is a life which must flood into our whole being, into the deepest depths and last abyss of our being, filling and transforming the whole world or realm of our personality.

Just as an empty cup put down into the sea is immersed and filled and no emptiness of any kind remains, so Love himself is to indwell us, that every thought in the conscious and subconscious mind is to be controlled by him, and every faculty that we possess is to be controlled and employed by him, not by force, but by our glad and willing cooperation, by our keeping every avenue open to him.

Love must rule in the whole realm of our individual personality, the whole world of our being must be under his control. Love must be king of the vast realms of our minds, that is to say of our complete thought life.

"The kingdom of God within you" (Luke 17:21). Not inside our bodies, but in every abyss and depth and level of our thought life. Love himself, thinking in us all the time, Love using our bodies through which to express himself.

"Thy kingdom come, thy will be done"— in me, as in heaven.

"As a man thinketh in his heart, so is he" (Prov. 23:7).

And surely the "heart" really means the inner immensity of my thought life, where will and choice and affection exercise their power and determine character. The spirit, or heart of me, is that part which thinks and wills and chooses, and therefore it is my thought life which controls and influences and rules my whole nature. It is the spiritual or thought realm as distinct from the material realm. It is the habits of my thought life which must be changed completely, and be brought under the full control of the King of Love, Jesus our Lord, whose Spirit of life dwells in me. The vast depths of my subconscious mind must be controlled by him too, and immense region of memory, of accumulated experience and knowledge, and that other vast and most creative of all areas, the imagination.

"The kingdom of God is within you." "Be ye transformed by the renewing of your mind" (Rom. 12:2). To be flooded with Love himself, reigning in me, until every thought and word and deed is love, that surely is salvation. His royal domain in which, and from which, and through which he exercises his will and control, is the heart or the thought life. He has taught us this himself (Matt. 12: 34-36; Matt. 15:17-20), most of all in his wonderful Sermon on the Mount in which he teaches us so clearly that all sin begins in the thought realm.

This new and glorious realization, when at last I experienced it, seemed completely overwhelming, but it was real and true, and it was possible, an invasion of my complete personality and thought life by the Spirit of Love himself in all his power. By this invasion of love I was to be transformed by a renewed mind. This was the glorious salvation he promised me, complete liberty and release from the tyranny of self reigning in my thought life.

The simile is perhaps not a very good one, but in actual fact, as this glorious realization gradually broke over me, I told myself with a delighted chuckle that I now knew exactly what a snake must feel like when it has at last slipped right out of its old skin, and in so doing got gloriously free of something that had become far too tight and narrow and ugly and depressing and imprisoning. For what prison and bondage is there so utterly dreary, indeed hideous, as the bondage of the thought life of a Christian still largely controlled by self, though all the time longing for deliverance.

What I began to experience now was a new

control altogether. It was no longer a question of doctrines and interpretations and Christian duties, and missionary activities, nor of agonizing longings to know how to love. No. I found that I had been as it were, annexed to heaven. And the King of Love who reigned in heaven now considered me a part of that realm over which he held sway.

It was like being invaded by a radiant, laughing army, love's army, who now came in to occupy newly acquired territory, yes, annexing me to heaven, as though my own little world of personality had been incorporated in the commonwealth of heaven. And the King of Love seemed to be saying with a glad laugh, "Now you have become part of a new universe altogether, the universe of love. And all you have to do now is to begin to explore it, and to revel in it."

The exact stages and steps by which this comparatively sudden and glorious climax was reached I shall try and describe in later chapters. But at that point what had been a dim vision and longing of my heart really became actual. As though clouds of mist which long had obscured the goal, although occasional breaks in the mist had already revealed to me ravishing peaks, or some brief glimpse of enchanting glory, now suddenly rolled away altogether, and lo, I was there, actually landed like a traveler from another world altogether, on a corner of the universe of love. And the King of that realm was welcoming me, and repeating again and again, "This is the realm of love. Begin to explore it."

# CHAPTER 3
# Exploration in The Realm of Love

"That Christ may dwell in your hearts by faith, that ye, being rooted and grounded in love, may be able to comprehend with all saints, what is the breadth and length, and depth and height, and to know the love of God which passeth knowledge, that ye might be filled with all the fullness of God" (Eph. 2:17-19).

"The invisible things of him from the creation of the world are clearly seen, being understood by the things that are made, even his eternal power and Godhead" (Rom. 1:20).

Soon after the time when this amazing inner experience took place, and I was landed in the universe of love and told to explore it, an almost similar experience happened in my outward life.

Utterly unexpectedly, as if out of the blue, I received a letter which was God's call to me to leave the mission field where I had worked for twenty years, and which started me off on what proved to be a long drawn-out journey around the whole world. As though the outward travel and exploration of this earthly world of ours was to be a type or picture of the travel and exploration which I was to undertake in the realm of love.

And so it came to pass that one Passover evening I took off by plane from the Lydda Airport in Israel, and all throughout the Easter weekend, which that year coincided with the Jewish Passover, I found myself flying through a cloudless sky, and looking down on the world to which the Lord our God once came to visit us in great humility, and where he had died for the deliverance of the whole of mankind.

We flew for hours over the utterly barren peninsula of Arabia, with its fantastic patterns of windblown, colored sands, and its occasional and unbelievably minute desert oases. Then over the Persian Gulf, with its submerged reefs of peacock blue and green, turquoise, amber and gold. We flew across the whole breadth of India from Karachi to Calcutta, looking down on a scene I could never have imagined.

I had read of the teeming multitudes in the villages of India, but had never even remotely pictured to myself the reality. For hour after hour, as I looked down from the plane, as far as the eye could reach in every direction, it seemed that where one village and its fields ended the next began. There seemed to be no wild, uncultivated land anywhere. Until, just before darkness fell, we found ourselves flying over a jumbled wilderness of never-ending mountains. When at last those were passed, then the villages and cities began again, this time visible only by their twinkling lights.

We flew on to Singapore, all down the Malay Straits, over Indonesia, circling twice above the immense, gaping crater of Bali; away over island after island, and sea after sea, until at last we reached the Antipodes, Australia and New Zealand. And over in that other hemisphere of the world for a whole year I traveled from place to place, a pilgrim indeed, gazing on many wonderful scenes which I had only read about or heard of, and many that I knew nothing about at all, but which I now saw for myself. The glaciers, snow peaks and amazing "bush" of western New Zealand, the immense sheep runs, the Blue Mountains of Australia and the Great

Barrier Reef; the coral islands in the Pacific Ocean, from Fiji and the New Hebrides, along the Solomon Islands and up to the steaming jungles of New Guinea.

I traveled by plane, train, motor, copra vessel, outrigger canoes and primitive open buses and vehicles of all kinds. Then I flew across the Pacific, had a look at the luxury hotels, swimming pools and beaches of Honolulu, and so came to Canada just as the daffodils, tulips and azaleas were bursting into bloom, while in the lands I had just left the trees were preparing to shed their leaves. I traveled through the indescribable glories of the Rocky Mountains, across the great Canadian prairies, bathed in the Muskoka lakes, and visited great cities in the United States, where I gazed with quite astonished admiration at their floodlit skyscrapers, towering up in beautiful tapering spires against the sky, and compared them with my memory of reed and grass huts; and the mud dwellings of Arab villages in Palestine.

I saw a never-ending kaleidoscope of form and color, beauty and ugliness, achievement and enterprise. And above all I met a multitude of people of every description, the makers, users and exploiters of all the products of those diverse realms which I had visited. Indians in saris and turbans, Chinese, Japanese, Maoris and Aboriginals, Solomon Islanders and Papuans in grass skirts and tattoo patterns, red Indians and pale-skinned peoples from almost all the na-

47

tions in the world.

As I traveled on, passing from place to place, certain things became real to my understanding as never before.

I began to realize in an absolutely new way how God loves the world, that is to say all these infinitely diverse peoples of the world; his passionate, absorbed interest in everything that goes on, above all, in every individual who lives on this planet. To him each and every one of them is a world in themselves; each individual character more diverse and vast and rich in potentiality and development than this material world and planet on which we live. And what men produce from the material products and possibilities of this earth is nothing in comparison with what can be produced in each one of these human worlds.

It came to me, too, with immense awe and thankfulness, that judging by the way he has created things God must have an intense love for, and interest in, diversity. It looks indeed as though he cannot bear uniformity, for every single thing he has made differs from everything else. There is not a single blade of grass exactly like another, nor snowflake, nor even the markings of the millions upon millions of our individual fingerprints.

There is certainly a general uniformity to special type or family, but even these types and families are almost too numerous to count. It would seem that the Eternal Creator revels, with the zest almost of great adventure, in producing diversity of every kind; though distortion, disharmony and marred beauty and perfection are no part of that diversity—they are defects to be overcome.

How stupid, how almost unbelievably stupid, we are if we imagine for one moment that he insists on uniformity in the thought realm, or that unity and uniformity are the same thing. How positively ridiculous to suppose that we must all express our worship in one form or pattern, or that he has one method which he prefers to another, or even that we must all understand exactly the same things about him. Sin and ugliness, selfishness and moral perversion, of course, must be abominable to him, but not diversity in love and obedience and understanding.

He has chosen thousands and thousands of different patterns, forms and shapes through which the plants, trees, fruits and flowers express his thoughts. Must the spiritual realm be that narrow and uniform? Is it not rather in the spiritual realm that we may expect and rejoice in the greatest diversity. All thoughts of the God of Love are creative; and where his own children are indwelt by his Spirit, his holy love, he will assuredly think and express a vast diversity of thoughts in and through them. Only they will all be in harmony with love. How then can we insist that all must be helped in one precise way, or come to have exactly the same thought patterns about God, or the same interpretations of the Scriptures.

His will for us all is that we should be "holy and without blame in love" (Eph. 1:4)—not that we should all be evangelicals, or for that matter liberals, or Protestants, or Roman Catholics, or anything else. We must not judge (pass sentence on one another, that our Lord himself has told us in Matt. 7:1-6), but we must distinguish by the spirit of holy love what is right and wrong for us. And, of course, the great moral laws are clear. We know the difference between right and wrong in the moral realm. This is implanted in our hearts, and in the commandments of God we have the rule of conduct, i.e., what actions are antagonistic to love.

In the Sermon on the Mount our Lord goes further, and shows us clearly what kinds of thought are antagonistic to love. Those thoughts and actions are wrong for everybody, because they are completely in disharmony with love. But there are multitudes of cases where we are prone to judge one another, where in reality what is perfectly right and legitimate for one, is quite wrong for another.

To give an extreme example, just as it is wrong for a fish to leave the water, and equally wrong for a hen to enter it, and right for both of them to revel in their own element, so in actual fact it appears to be perfectly right for some temperaments to express their love and praise to Christ by shouting, all praying aloud together, clapping their hands, singing the same thing over and over again, and even sometimes to lie on the floor, whereas for another temperament to join in this abandonment would be the most shocking and unbecoming way of manifesting their worship.

On the other hand, the former type would feel it an intolerable insult to their Lord to try and worship in an atmosphere of cold formality. The unfortunate results happen when people are mistakenly convinced that the only way to the blessing they long for lies in one certain type of worship which cannot, in actual fact, help them.

How many people have given up going to church altogether because the form they had been brought up in proved for them intolerably boring, or cold or lifeless. Whereas others have been persuaded that real spiritual power is only to be achieved through an utter abandonment, which in their case is entirely unsuitable, and only produces hysteria and even worse features.

How much more wise and happy it must be to seek, if necessary, until we do find the form which makes it most easy and natural and joyful to express our praise and love and worship, and then gladly use that way, and rejoice in the countless different forms through which God's other children find the same blessing.

There is one glorious unity, the unity of conformity to the Creator's will for each one of us individually, through a complete yielding of our whole personality to him, and living in an attitude of joyful responsiveness to his Holy Spirit. For in reality we are all different worlds, made up of just as varied continents or realms, seas and islands, heights and depths, climates and temperatures, powers and potentialities, as the most variegated world imaginable. And it is only when love, which is our response to the Creator, reigns in the kingdom of our own world and personality that we can be brought into real harmony and unity with the whole universe of other human spirits.

The other thing which I came to understand as never before is that God, our Creator, must be extraordinarily interested in overcoming evil, that the only conceivable reason why he permits it to continue to exist is that it may be overcome, that it will be overcome, and transformed into something else. Indeed it would seem that this is the one supreme reason why such a world as this planet Earth was created, and this physical and mortal life, among material things, was planned for us.

We are born into this physical realm that we may learn to overcome. To overcome the difficulties and tests and conditions forced upon us by such immense varieties in climate, temperature, productivity of the soil, and such challenging physical hazards as conquest of the sea, and air, of mountain peaks and arctic zones, equatorial heats, wild jungle, barren deserts, swamps, germs, parasites, heat and cold, hunger and thirst, hardness and perils of every kind. But above all to learn, through these physical symbols of the spiritual, to overcome in the moral realm. And the things that we have overcome will be the things which accompany us into eternal life.

For example, what is real joy, the joy which cannot be taken from us, but sorrow accepted and transformed. What is real peace, but struggle and strife, fear and anxiety overcome. What indeed is real love but self love overcome and transformed into a passion for self-giving. And probably we shall find that every experience of trial, difficulty and suffering, of wrong done to us and accepted and forgiven, all these things will have worked in us some lovely trophy for eternity. "He that overcometh shall inherit all things." And perhaps the accepted and overcome evils will be found to have been transformed into the precious jewels of which the New Jerusalem is built (Rev. 21:18-27).

We are here in order that, as sons of God through our Lord Jesus Christ, and by his life given to us, we may become creative love thinkers, willers and doers of good.

So it seemed to me that wherever I went traveling around the world it was indeed like the outward and visible map of an inner journey being made in the invisible world, the realm of love. And compared to the things in that realm the greatest glories and beauties of this earth fade into nothingness.

It is true that now we only see or understand the beauties of that invisible realm as through a glass darkly, rather like tourists gazing through their dark glasses at the glories of dazzling snow peaks, almost blinded by the radiance, and able at present only to explore the outermost fringes of the spiritual world; but nevertheless waiting for the time when, this mortal body left behind, we may advance even further and further into that glory.

Even now the kingdom of God is to be realized within us, in our renewed minds, as more and more fully we come under the reign and rule of the King of Love, Christ Jesus our Lord; and in that way brought into an ever-developing unity—though not uniformity—with all other human beings who have already surrendered themselves to the law of love, and the King of Love, or who long to do so.

# CHAPTER 4
# Enemies of Love

"This kind goeth not forth but by prayer and fasting."

If the spirit of love is really born in you, you know it by the price you have paid for it in the many deaths to self which you have suffered, before the spirit of love came to life in you" (William Law).

I will now try to describe the way by which I was brought into the kingdom of love. Nobody has exactly the same experience, but sometimes hearing of the way in which others have been led can be a real help, and the very fact that it was so long before I found the key into that kingdom leads me to think that perhaps there are others who long to enter into that glorious experience, who yet, like myself, cannot find the way.

I had known all through the years of my Christian life that I desperately needed victory over certain besetting sins, and escape from the bondage of certain habits, that I needed to have occasional victory changed into permanent victory. Above all, that I needed to love. But what I had never clearly realized all through those years was that the kingdom of God is within us, and is in actual fact centered in our thought life. What we are there is what we are actually. "As man thinketh in his heart, so is he." And that, of course, is why none of us can claim to be different or better than others by nature, because of the appalling things which we discover harbored in our thought life, things which we would have thought ourselves incapable of thinking.

And somehow, though I knew only too well that my thought life was a chaotic wilderness of wrong thoughts, some so horrible, I just couldn't imagine how they had appeared there, and of cultivated areas, as it were, where the right kind of thoughts were produced, I just did not realize that the whole secret of loving lies here, in the thought realm.

I knew that it was quite true that it was not what we say or do, but what we are that really counts, but somehow I never really understood that what we are depends entirely upon what we think. Our habits of thought make us the kind of people we are. So it was that when I was not actually praying and reading the Bible and preaching, all too often I was practicing thought habits which were proud, selfish and terribly critical of others.

Half of my thought life, thank God, was controlled by the Lord I loved. But much of the time, in actual fact, it wasn't. I knew this and grieved over it, but for all those years I could not find the way of escape. The old, natural habits of a lifetime bound me so fast, like fetters on a prisoner, which were loosed for several hours a day and then riveted back again. As all thought habits are literally creative, it is they which create our words and actions and manner. Everything we do and are springs from our habitual thought patterns.

I knew to my sorrow and shame that, though people would often be helped through my preaching, if they had to live with me and work with me, the helpful influence of my preaching would often be lost, because they would not like me in ordinary everyday life. I used to tell myself, "I just can't help being ungracious and irritable, much as I detest it. I don't know why, but people do irritate me so terribly that I just can't help reacting ungraciously." What I really meant, without realizing it, was "If I live with them, I am afraid that people will see through me into my mind, where I really am in bondage with critical, unloving thoughts about them."

Yet, of course, the truth was that people could not really see through me into my mind, but that these detestable, unloving thoughts would force themselves out in spite of all my efforts to keep them shut up in my mind and invisible to others, and insist on expressing themselves in words and through my ungracious manner and actions. We don't really see through people, but they make their inner thoughts visible in a thousand ways, however carefully they may guard their lips. For as we think so we are and we just can't hide it for long. When we have been yielding our minds to Christ and talking to him, we also cannot fail to reveal it in some way afterwards. Thank God for this true and comforting thought.

The thoughts controlled by the Holy Spirit "will out," just as much as the other kind of self-thoughts, and that is why we are often such an extraordinary mixture of Christian and un-Christian in our life and witness, until we find the glorious release of those who come to know the reign of God within them all the time. This it is which explains our up-and-down experience, and why for years, perhaps, we know victory at times and failure at others. As we have been thinking—so we are.

We know our friends and acquaintances by what they unconsciously reveal of their inner habits of the thought life. And the compassionate remark made by real friends, "What a pity that Hannah, with all her earnestness, has such an ungracious, irritable and critical temperament," means in simple truth, "What a pity Hannah so often thinks ungracious, irritable and critical thoughts about others." Just as those who definitely dislike her, when they dub her "the proud Miss Hurnard," simply express the horrible truth that Miss Hurnard obviously thinks a great deal about herself and can't hide it.

Whereas, of course, if one never allows irritated, annoyed, critical or unloving thoughts to remain in the mind a moment, however strongly they may clamor for permission to remain, and if only creative love thinking is the habit of our thought life, nobody will be able to see through us or in us, thoughts that are not there, and our whole outward manner will be transformed.

Of course this does not mean that we shall cease to notice things that are wrong or weak or faulty, or annoying in others, or force ourselves to condone them, or try to justify them as though they did not matter just because they appear in others and not in ourselves. Love is not blind. Indeed the standard of love is so high that we shall be more conscious than ever before of what comes short of love, and of what may stumble others.

The difference, however, will be in our mental reaction to the people who manifest these things. Irritation, anger and dislike will be cast back the moment they clamor to rush in and the thought reaction of the Holy Spirit of love within us will be concentrated, not on the ugly or exasperating or unfortunate blemish, but on the very opposite quality. That is to say we shall treat the ugly fact creatively, just as our Lord did, with love's creative power, allowing love to use our imagination to picture that person healed and completely delivered from the blemish and radiantly transformed. As, for example, the Lord did when he so plainly saw Peter's exasperating instability and foolish impetuosity and said, "You will become a rock."

Then we shall turn this lovely thought picture of the person as the Lord means to make them, into prayer (refusing with determination even to recall the blemish in them, because that has such a bad effect upon ourselves and our attitude towards them), and we shall join our Lord in asking that the perfect picture thus held in our thoughts shall become real in that person's experience. Intercession itself of course is thinking under the Lord's control, allowing ourselves to be shown the ideal which he wants, in ourselves and in others, and joining with him in praying and claiming that it shall come to pass. But I shall be considering this more fully in the chapter, "Creative Love Thinking."

I began to realize all this very clearly indeed, and saw that salvation must mean this complete deliverance and healing of the whole personality, a transformation in fact, through the renewing of our minds; a release from the slavery of self into the perfect liberty and creative power, with the ability to overcome evil and transform it into good, which becomes the experience of those who live under the control of perfect love. The kingdom of heaven within us must be the reign of holy love. But though I began to realize it, I still could not see how it could become my own experience. Pray and struggle as long as I might, I simply could not reach the place where every thought was brought into captivity to the King of Love, so that every word and deed was an expression of his love.

Like Paul and a countless multitude of Christians in every age, I could only cry out despairingly, "O wretched being that I am, who shall deliver me from the body of this death?"—this life of wanting to do good, and finding evil present with me all the time. "For to will is present with me, but how to perform that which is good, I find not" (Rom. 7:8-21).

As one reads the writings and experiences of Christians in all ages, one cannot help realizing that, though this experience is common to all, it would seem that in every generation the actual experience of entering into the deliverance which our Lord Jesus gives varies very greatly. And I think that one of our chief difficulties is that we suppose that the same formula which helped others in an earlier generation must be the formula for our age too. Whereas in this also our Lord seems to love great variety, and if we cannot find this blessed experience, "I thank God through Jesus Christ," in the same way as our fathers found it, it simply means that we shall find it in some other way.

I had been nurtured on the writings of the great evangelicals, and had read with prayerful and envious longing the experiences of these great Christians, and how they too finally, and with a joy which was overwhelming, had entered into this blessing. I knew how John and Charles Wesley had found it, and Hudson Taylor and Henrietta Soltau, and Dr. F. B. Meyer and many others. And I had read literally dozens of books on the subject of being filled with the Spirit, and books on holiness, as well as listening to scores of addresses on the subject. But none of them seemed able to help me beyond increasing my longing for such an experience. I could not find the way to experience it, and their way when I tried to follow it simply did not work in my own case.

They all seemed to emphasize that the Holy Spirit in all his fullness was to be received by faith alone, by a simple childlike acceptance of the fact that God had promised to give him to us if we asked for him and were willing to surrender to him. When we had confessed all known sin, and asked God for him, we were to believe that he had come in, quite apart from all feelings, and were to thank him in faith. I followed this formula many times, most earnestly and sincerely, but in my case the expected result did not follow. It seemed that I must have left out some vital ingredient.

In the same way I read and heard that to be crucified with Christ was simply to believe or reckon that I was dead to sin, that the old self was actually dead, through the merit of efficacy of the death of Christ, and by identifying myself with that death. But reckon as I might, and believe as I sincerely did in the atoning death of Christ, the dreadful fact remained that I did not become dead to sin. Far from it. Along would come the next temptation or provocation or exasperation, irritability, or my own special besetting sin (which I shall mention in a minute), and I was no more dead to self than I ever had been, but terribly and horribly alive.

Again and again self proved overwhelmingly stronger than my will, able to smash through every barrier I had tried to set up of self-control, reckoning the old life to be a corpse, yes, and even calling upon the Lord to deliver me. (How good it is that he will not answer even such prayers for victory in temptation until we are brought at last through repeated failure to see or understand just where the source of failure really lies.) I went on committing myself to him again and again—I was no stranger to heart-searching and full and earnest surrender (no really sincere evangelicals are), but the formula which I had always believed to be right failed in my case.

For a long time I thought that it was my besetting sins themselves which needed to be surrendered, and then I would be delivered from their power. But though I surrendered my irritable temper again and again, nothing happened. I tried to drag all my old enemies to the cross and ask the Lord to crucify them (just as the books all seemed to urge me to do). But that didn't work either. With my will I would yield them and condemn them, over and over again. But it was like a judge sitting in the court when the judgment was given, but still needing to be captured.

And then at last I realized that it was not just yielding these besetting sins themselves that was necessary, but I must find the secret hoarded keys which opened the gates and let these enemies into the kingdom of my thought realm. And that was quite a different matter. How could the keys be found?

Now there was one particular habit in my life which was very destructive and absolutely wrong for a disciple of the Lord Jesus, but I just could not overcome it, nor get free. It was a habit I had indulged in all my life, even from the time that I was a morbid, unhappy child, with such a bad stammer that I was incapable of making friends, or facing up to life in any way. It was the habit of day-dreaming—with myself in the center of the pictures.

At first it was a way of escape from reality. Afterwards I continued to indulge in it as a pleasant and delightful way of relaxation. Until now I could by no means break the habit. And yet I felt quite sure that in some way it was the main cause of all my failure and inability to love. Though I could not for the life of me see why it should be so, yet the whole habit produced a guilty feeling in me.

At this point the Lord reminded me of a remark made by the principal of the Bible college where I had trained. She had said, "If anyone is prone to indulge in daydreaming delightfully about themselves, if they carefully watch themselves afterwards they will always find that they are behaving irritably and disagreeably towards other people."

That remark, as I now recalled it, seemed somehow to be probing painfully near to the core of my trouble. But why should it be so. I couldn't see the connection. Why should daydreaming always produce irritability? And then, suddenly I saw it. Because the act of "burning incense" before self in this way, namely enthroning self in the center of the stage of imagination, is inescapably certain to puff one up with an inflated feeling of superiority. In my daydreams I was always the heroine—a gracious, charming, gifted yet humble heroine, whom others delighted to honor. And there it was, as clear as crystal before me, that was where the proud, superior Miss Hurnard evolved from.

"As a man thinketh in his heart, so is he." And if a woman always sees herself as a very superior and gracious heroine on the screen of her imagination, very unpleasantly superior and ungracious she will be in actual life, as soon as she emerges from that inner, secret picture show, especially when in contact with people who behave toward her quite differently from those she had been visualizing mentally!

I now saw the key for which I was looking, and I exclaimed in horror, "I see now that I am always irritable and annoyed with other people and uninterested in them, and prone to despise them, first, when I have been gossiping about them to other people, and secondly when I have been showing off myself and drawing attention to my own virtues. And most of all and always, when I have been daydreaming about myself." And then I added despairingly: "But I can't stop daydreaming, Lord. It's impossible. When the temptation comes, I just give in at once."

Then he made me consider the question: When did the temptation to daydream come? Not when I was reading my Bible, or preaching, or visiting, or teaching, and certainly not when I was talking to the Lord. The temptation always came when I was free to relax, in my free time, and when on holiday. And always without fail after I had been reading a novel or a magazine, for every new story started me off putting myself in the place of the heroine, and creating a whole new serial or film in my imagination.

There was the key. I was passionately fond of reading, and I remembered the Lord's words, "If thine eye or hand offend, cut it off." And I saw what I must do. I must stop reading altogether (at least temporarily, and very likely for always) any sort of book which would encourage this habit, and that meant all works of fiction, even good ones, and every secular magazine. It seemed horribly drastic, but quite clear. I must cut off everything which would stimulate daydreaming, and substitute for it only such reading as would increase my knowledge, and above all, help me to love and understand my Lord better.

I knew many missionaries who would say that such a drastic fast would make me very one-sided and unbalanced and out of touch with life. For them that might be true; but for me the key to my individual failure was discovered, and I could either hand it over to the Lord, or decide not to make the sacrifice, and so go on in bondage. I saw even then, and later came to experience, that the four things went together. This was the "fast" which the Lord asked of me personally. I was to fast completely from criticizing other people, and from talking about my own victories, and from reading fiction, and from daydreaming. If I kept this fourfold fast all the gates would be safely locked. If I broke one of them, I would again find myself powerless. And so I found it.

When that surrender was made, and that fourfold fast entered upon, for the first time in my life I immediately found myself delivered from the habit of daydreaming, able to refrain from criticizing others, and from the very desire to do so, indeed a great horror of it was born in me; moreover, I found that my critical, impatient thoughts were now completely changed and my whole attitude toward other people transformed, just as I have described in the earlier chapters. For I was really and truly set down in the universe of love, and in my thought realm I was transformed by the renewing of my mind. The thing I had prayed for so long actually happened, not gradually, but immediately. I knew that the kingdom of love had come within, because the gates were shut and locked against love's enemies.

Some people, perhaps, will feel that this experience savors of preaching works and not grace, that it was a struggle to overcome. Not so—far from it, it was a letting go at last of the secret keys, my own individual cause of failure. Then the grace and deliverance was instantaneous, and it was the Lord himself, the King of Love, who then delivered me from all my enemies and garrisoned my mind.

Some of us just cannot be delivered because deep down somewhere within we are not willing to be shown exactly what it is we must be delivered from. It is so much easier, and far less humbling, to give it the general name of sin, and ask to be delivered from that. But it won't do. It is my sin, my own special besetting sin, which I must be released from. And when that is recognized and confessed, then the cleansing and delivering power is given. But this kind truly goeth not forth but by prayer and fasting.

It is simply impossible to describe the radiant joy and release which instantaneously followed the slaying of this old enemy monster which had devastated my thought life for so long, tyrannous habit of a lifetime —daydreaming—the one thing above all others from which I had thought I could not be delivered until released from the body itself. But it seems that the slaying of that evil thing was the key to the whole problem, and when that was dealt with and destroyed, then at once I could begin to love, and know that the prayer I had so often prayed was being answered at last.

# CHAPTER 5
# Love
# Accepting

"I delight to do thy will, O My God." "In acceptance lieth peace." "Go through every day praising for everything."

When once I had entered into this glorious experience of finding the kingdom of love within me because love reigns throughout the whole thought life, transforming it through the renewing of my mind, I began to make discoveries. I found that there are definite principles to be followed and obeyed in the kingdom of love, and these principles are of vital importance in controlling our relationship with all other Christians, especially those with whom we disagree, whose point of view we fear or distrust, or whose personalities we find uncongenial or difficult.

These principles form, as it were, a very simple but utterly tremendous alphabet, or ABC, of love. We begin to learn to spell out this alphabet slowly and painfully, as soon as we become disciples of Christ. But as we learn it more fully and fluently, this alphabet is used by the Holy Spirit of love to form a language by which he is able to express himself in our lives, and to make us what the apostle Paul terms "living epistles, read and known of all men." I would like to share very simply in the next three chapters some of the lessons I have been learning through the simple ABC's of love, or the three chief principles which love writes in the very hearts of those he reigns in.

Love accepts with joy all that God's will permits to happen to us.

Love bears and forgives all that others do to us.

Love creates goodness through creative love thinking.

Our Lord summed up the whole nature of love in the one commandment that he gave us, "That ye love one another as I have loved you." We shall find that these are the three principles of love which he himself followed.

The first was that he accepted with joy all that God permitted to happen to him. His whole attitude from first to last was a joyous and radiant, "I delight to do thy will, O my God." Whatever came to him through the circumstances he was involved in, and above all, through what other people (his disciples as well as his enemies) did to him, he received with praise and thanksgiving.

This, then, must also be the first great purpose and principle of our lives, learning to accept every single thing which God allows to happen to us, and to react towards it creatively. When once we are willing to accept the truth that there are no second causes at all, and that we have been set down in this world and given this human experience, on purpose that we may meet and overcome evil, and difficulty, sin and sorrow, then obviously the only right attitude of heart is this attitude which our Lord had all the time, "I delight to do (and to accept) thy will, O my God."

Remember that an attitude of heart is actually a state of mind, the habit of our thought life. We are often so slow to realize this and tell ourselves vaguely that it means our feeling and affections, forgetting that our feelings and affections may often be quite different from our will or our real longings, and also that both feelings and affections can eventually be changed and modified by our thoughts.

Learning to delight in whatever God permits to happen to us, however unattractive, hard, unjust, cruel, unbearable or wrong it may seem to be, and even though it seems to be caused by the wrongdoing of others, or their lack of love, or even through spite and malice, is the first great lesson which love would have us learn.

This, of course, does not mean that we are to submit passively to sin, evil or temptation, or that we are to accept what God does not will for us, in the sense of saying to ourselves, "God has let this happen, so there is nothing I can do about it but submit." Nor does it mean that we are to take no part in helping and delivering others in their difficult or oppressive circumstances. But it does mean that under no circumstances whatsoever may we feel resentful or sorry for ourselves, or react with bitterness and unwillingness to forgive. Love must always react creatively, destroying the wrong or evil situation by overcoming it with good—never, no never, using bad means to destroy it, or the same methods which the evil one uses.

It does mean too that we may never seek to evade, or escape from, these events or happenings, but to accept them all as trials and tests which have a definite purpose, namely, that we should use them as the stuff or material out of which to fashion our character for the glory of God. Submission is good if it is the best we can achieve at first, but it can be a very negative and uncreative thing. Whereas accepting with joy is one of the most creative and liberating experiences that we can know.

It is through accepting the circumstances that come to us in life that self is crucified. There is no other way. No reckoning of ourselves as dead to sin can avail anything unless we reckon, or accept the fact, that we have no right to resent anything which is done to us, but that our right is to react to everything in a creative way by using it to express and manifest love in some way.

How easily we murmur and complain at certain things which happen to us in life! We feel so sorry for ourselves, forgetting that the great sin of the children of Israel was just this very attitude, namely, murmuring against God. As Christians we tell ourselves that, of course, we are not murmuring against God, certainly not, we would never dream of such a thing! What we are complaining about is the way life has ill-treated us, the undeserved frustrations and trials which we have met, and the way our fellow human beings have misunderstood and wronged us, and we feel we are justified in resenting it.

We ignore this great truth, that there are no second causes, any more than there were in the life of wronged and persecuted Joseph. All that happens to us (even the results of our own folly, stupidity and sin, as well as the results of the follies, stupidities and sins of others), all constitute a God-permitted opportunity to bring good out of evil.

The New Testament emphasizes and underlines this truth over and over again. "Rejoicing in tribulation." "We glory in necessities and infirmities." "My brethren, count it all joy." And our Lord's own injunction, "Blessed are ye when men shall revile you and persecute you, and shall say all manner of evil against you falsely, for my name's sake. Rejoice and be exceeding glad."

Oswald Chambers insisted that almost the worst sin of all is self-pity. He says that it makes us "spit out complaints" against God, and causes us to become "craving spiritual sponges" always wanting to sop up sympathy, and resentful when it is not given! I have been enormously helped and blessed by one simple sentence of advice which seems to sum up this first principle of creative love, and which, if practiced, really has the power to turn life into a song from beginning to end.

Go through each day praising for everything, for the seemingly bad and cruel and heartbreaking experiences which come to us personally (not to others), as well as for the obviously good and delightful things, remembering that it is not the things which happen to us, but our reaction to them which is important; and it is by seeking to react always in love that the kingdom of God reveals its presence within us.

I began to learn this tremendous principle through one of the most difficult and yet lovely experiences which has come to me in life. But though I began to learn it as a young Christian, I did not seem able to practice it all the time (as I have already related) in the little trials of life as well as the big ones, until I realized that when we are baptized into love, this is the first character in love's alphabet. This is the experience:

While I was still a comparatively young Christian, I was brought much against my will into a set of completely new circumstances and relationships, which to the very depths of my heart I felt I could not face nor go through with. This experience came to me without any warning of any kind, entirely unexpected and completely unavoidable. And I had to face the question, how should I react to it? What attitude should I as a Christian take in such a situation? A situation which I honestly felt was a wrong one and not according to God's will.

In theory I knew, of course, what the Christian attitude should be—love at all costs and the complete abasement of self (though I did not at that time understand anything about the creative power of self-abasement and self-giving). But in an actual, and frightfully real experience, I found myself wallowing, indeed almost swallowed up, in a flood of the most terrible resentment, bitterness and humiliation.

Never can I forget with what a horror of anguish and shame I prayed for weeks on end to be delivered from these hateful feelings. I knew that they were a complete contradition to everything I had been taught, that to give way to them with my will would be like denying my Lord, and crucifying him all over again. Never once did he allow me to give way to them with my will, but somehow I could not escape from their clutch.

The sensations and feelings of resentment and bitterness would come sweeping over me like an irresistible wave, and while they lasted each time, there I was, battered and hating myself, yet clinging to the Lord, telling him I detested these feelings, that I trusted him to save me from them, insisting that he enable me to meet them triumphantly, and as more than victor over them; even reminding him again and again that his name was Jesus, Savior, and that he was called Jesus because he promised to save his people from their sins, and that if he could not save wicked, hateful me in this unexpected and apparently overwhelming situation, and make me victorious in love, he was not worthy of his name, and that I would never be able to preach again to anyone that he was a Savior who could save to the uttermost. That if he didn't prove his power now I was lost.

But all the time the ideal of what Christ wanted and expected was never shaken. He kept it before me like a steadfast beacon. He insisted on nothing less than the very attitude which would be his own under similar circumstances. That was the standard to which he pledged himself to bring me.

During the earlier weeks of this tempest-tossed period I went up again to the Lake District to attend the Keswick Convention. And one day, when I was nearly in despair over the turmoil in my heart, as I thought of facing the ordeal which lay ahead, I went off to the Fells alone, and, sitting among the heather, tried to think out what course I ought to take. Should I follow my own feelings and desire and let it be known, as nicely as possible, that I felt it would be easier and happier for all concerned if I gave up all idea of trying to make the best of an impossible situation, and one which I expected to irk my pride so intolerably? I could flounce away from the situation altogether, refuse to face it, and make my escape into an independent life.

It was a grey, misty morning, and the tops of the Fells all around me were shrouded in cloud. Suddenly, straight ahead of me, on the other side of a deep valley, a rent appeared in the clouds, and I found myself looking up another valley in the mountains opposite. And over on that side the sun was shining, so that the country between the curtains of cloud gleamed like a jewel. There were green slopes and purple heather, and misty blues and mauves and gold, shining land, full of glory, and with no clouds or darkness. And before the clouds closed in again and shut out that radiant little bit of a kingdom of light, the Lord spoke to me as clearly and gently as possible:

"You could react like that, Hannah, and flounce away, but it would shut you out of my kingdom and make you an exile from the place where I reign." And then he added words from the Bible which I had hardly noticed before,

"Behold, I show you a better way, the way of love."

All my life since then I have cherished like a jewel that little phrase which so suddenly shone into my dark, troubled mind, "A better way, the way of love."

I cried out, however, at once, "But Lord, I can't walk that way. It isn't that I don't want to, it is simply that I can't. I want to love, and I want to act lovingly, but I fail the whole time because I don't feel loving. I feel only furious and hurt and humiliated and wanting to escape. And my nerves can't bear the strain. I feel at breaking point all the time. I want to follow the way of love, but I don't believe I could even crawl along it on my hands and knees in this case. It is beyond me." And he said:

"It is better to go stumbling and weeping and crawling like a worm along the way of love than to give it up and choose some other way."

And so I started crawling, literally crawling, along the way of love, inwardly weeping a great deal, and stumbling most of the time because I felt so sorry for myself, but learning for the first time that love, real love, is not primarily a feeling at all, but a thing of the will. A determination to act as I would if I felt all the delight of loving deeply and happily. For I found that if one acts in love, sooner or later one comes to feel all the joy and ecstasy of love.

Some people have the idea that it is really hypocritical to act toward others as if we really loved them, when in reality we may only feel dislike or shrinking, and actually disapprove of what they are doing. And that if we continue to act outwardly as though we love them, we generally have ulterior motives, and wish to keep in with them for some personal gain. I can only say from experience that prayerfully and earnestly desiring to love a person, and trying to act lovingly towards them at a time when we do not feel love, but perhaps just the opposite, is in actual fact crawling along the way of love. If persisted in, it will, without doubt, bring us right through the painful, crawling, groveling stage into the radiant, joyous, almost exuberant stage of running along the way of love.

It is never hypocrisy to act as we earnestly desire to feel, even though the feeling may be very contrary at the time. And if perhaps someone is acting in a way we really disapprove of, or feel to be quite wrong, we shall need to love all the more in order to be able to help them, even when they persist in the wrong action. As it happened, in this particular case the situation did not prove to be wrong after all, but opened up to me one of the happiest and richest relationships in my life, little as I expected it.

But even when one really longs and wills to overcome the lack of love in one's own heart, it is only when the path to real self-crucifixion is followed in actual fact, and through the actual daily submission to the thing we so dread or dislike or fear, that victory can be given. When once we face up to it, and take the first, perhaps agonizing, steps in going through with it, then we find the supposed impossibility melts away.

I remember standing in the corridor of the train as it approached the place where I was to go through my ordeal, shaking from head to foot, and telling myself desperately that I simply could not face it, and then crying out to the Lord, "Must I really go? Can't you let me off this hurting humiliating experience? I will love, really I will, if only I may stay away, but if I go into this thing it will be a dreadful failure, because I'm just not capable of dealing with it."

And my Lord said, "There is just one secret of success, Hannah; you must accept it with joy, and determine to go all lengths in yielding every right. If you make even one reservation in your mind it will mean failure. Yield everything. You have no rights at all in this situation, only the right to love and help. Rejoice in that. And if you once say to yourself over any single point, 'That is too much to ask,' 'no one can expect that of me,' 'I must just be allowed that one remaining privilege,' or even 'it would not be right to give in all the time,' failure will be certain."

The train slowed down in the station, and I went out to meet the impossible situation with this thought ringing in my mind as a warning and a challenge.

"Go all lengths. Remember, no reservations."

And what happened? There was a certain amount of pain at first, and sometimes even the tiny details of going all lengths felt quite impossible. But when attempted, the impossibility dissolved, and joy rushed in. And, moreover, I was humbled greatly by finding that on the other side, too, there was exactly the same determination to go all lengths in showing love and kindness and humility, and that in a situation which must have been harder even than my own.

It is quite impossible to describe the blessing and enrichment which have come to me through this experience, which I felt at the time was all wrong, and which, when I accepted it because it was permitted by God, turned out to be a special joy and comfort to me ever since, and in some ways a friendship more enriching than any others I have known.

But supposing it had not turned out so? What if, for instance, the others concerned had chosen to go all lengths in making things difficult and trying to cause suffering? Such things do happen, even among Christians. Even then, the principle still holds good.

Accept that too with the joy of knowing that even through such circumstances God will bring perhaps even greater enrichment. For the greater the evil, the greater the opportunity to fashion out of it everlasting good. There are no circumstances allowed to come into the lives of God's own children which cannot be transformed into ultimate blessing. God will not allow anything to happen to us which can only harm us and is incapable of being transformed into enrichment. "For we know that all things work together for good, to them that love God . . ." (Rom. 8:28).

Whereas if resentment and bitterness and self-pity are harbored in our hearts and we refuse to accept what God permits, and continually struggle against it, or seek to evade the challenge and to face the test, then spiritual, mental and physical impoverishment will follow. There is no prison house so cruel as the prison of resentment and self-pity, and the effect on those who languish long in that bondage is to suffer a progressively destructive influence on character, personality and physical health. Our Lord warns us about this in the most solemn manner possible, "Verily I say unto thee, thou shalt by no means come out thence, till thou hast paid the uttermost farthing" (Matt. 5:26).

It should only be during the earlier years of our Christian life that the battles in the realm of the mind or spirit should have to be fought out in the gloom and darkness and passionate feeling which was natural to the old nature. As our Lord takes over control of more and more of the realm of the mind, so the dark and cloudy periods should become more and more rare, for darkness belongs to sin.

As with the creation of the earth, so with the new creation in our spirits, the evening and the morning make up the day. First, there is the darkness and chaos of self's dominion, and then the dawning into the full light and sunshine of perfect day. Outwardly our circumstances may be gloomy and dark indeed, but more and more the inner reaction to these difficulties and trials will be one of joy and peace. Temptations and trials do not get less difficult, indeed the maturer the spiritual development the sterner the tests, but we are children of the light, and the kingdom of light will extend more and more fully over the whole heart and mind, until we come so completely under the reign of love that every thought and every reaction will be love only.

Obviously, all through life there will be circumstances and times in which it is easy to rejoice, and others in which it will be far, far harder. There will be times of special testing when we shall be called upon to prove our willingness to delight in the will of God for us, even though it means Gethsemane and a cross. But if we have allowed the Holy Spirit of love to keep us praising every day for everything, the small and comparatively insignificant trials as well as the big ones, we shall find that he can do the same for us in the midst of the fiery, burning furnace of affliction, pain and sorrow.

Certainly the hardest circumstances of all must be undergone by those held captive in the hands of cruel enemies, imprisoned, starved and tortured, until the whole body is weakened almost beyond endurance. But there is abundant evidence that even under those circumstances, if not at once, at any rate eventually, the very richest, highest and most glorious experiences of the Christian life become possible.

There are some who have been able to rise to higher heights of love and devotion than they would have thought possible when living under easier circumstances. One has only to think of Bunyan, incarcerated for years in the stinking Bedford Jail, and enabled to write *The Pilgrim's Progress* there, which after the Bible, is the greatest book of all time, and is full of a radiant imagination as well as of beautiful spiritual emotion, to realize the heavenly climate he dwelt in, even under such circumstances. For the kingdom of God in the realm of his mind was flooding him with joy, and peace and love.

But it is the same in our day and generation, and in a little book called, I think, *In the Valley of the Shadow*, written by one of the pastors who was a prisoner for years in the hands of the Gestapo, we have a wonderful and beautiful example of what suffering and tribulation have brought to an ever-increasing number of God's children in this twentieth century. For many months he had been hungry, almost perishing with the cold in winter, and enduring long spells of solitary confinement, expecting every hour to be taken from his cell and hanged or shot. He tells us how he was enabled to learn step by step to accept "the holy and difficult will of God," and found that it brought him the supreme joy and fulfillment of his life.

What he learned while suffering at the hands of the Gestapo was so wonderful an experience of the love and grace of God, that he almost dreaded freedom, lest, under easier circumstances, he should lose that experience. He writes as follows in a chapter called "Hallowed Suffering:"

"My cell was only five paces wide . . . but in those silent days of autumn, when the sun shone through the bars, it had something of the austere beauty of a monk's cell . . . The stream of time flowed on quietly and majestically towards God . . . In those days it was granted me to tread the shores of that land which lies on the outermost fringe of time, upon which already something of the radiance of the other world is shining . . . an existence which, though still earthly and human, was open to the world of God.

"I had to go down step by step into the depths . . . It was the sense of utter helplessness which enabled me to throw myself upon the mercy of God . . . I had to struggle to overcome the fear of death. Here again it was the same sense of utter helplessness. I said to myself, 'like this cell and these fetters, here is something I cannot evade, there is only one way to the mercy of God, and that is that I must seek it at the point which He Himself will show me. Only if I willingly surrender to His holy will can I praise Him . . .'

"Henceforth I looked up daily to the Son of God, Who in the Garden of Gethsemane had surrendered to the difficult and holy will of God, and through His agony and conflict robbed death of its fears. From Him I learned to endure trembling and anguish, and to say yes to this difficult and holy will of God. This is an agony upon which God's blessing rests, a holy fire which burns away one's guilt . . . I began to understand that God can only reveal this to a man who is in the depths of suffering. Hence one whom God has led into this school of knowledge can only praise Him for the experience, as the most wonderful spiritual gift which he has ever received."

Yes, it is a well-proved fact that the kingdom of love can come to greater perfection in the heart and minds of those who suffer greatly than under easier circumstances. But there are not many of us who are called to walk the martyr's path. And strangely enough in our own more everyday experience, it seems easier to rise to the occasion when the test is great, perhaps almost over-whelming, than to live in the climate of heaven in ordinary and exasperating daily circumstances. It seems harder to meet the almost hourly frets and irritations and per-haps irksome tasks of home or business with unbroken praise and thankfulness and love.

We know that the Lord has commanded us to love our enemies and bless our perse-cutors, but it sometimes seems quite a dif-ferent matter to treat our fellow Christians who may prove uncongenial, uncooperative, self-opinionated and unloving, in the same way, perhaps because we tell ourselves that they really ought to know better. But it is in the everyday life and circumstances of each one of us that the reign of love must come. "Let this mind be in you which was in Christ Jesus." This is the "A" of love's alphabet. Accept with joy. "In acceptance lieth peace."

"Go through each day praising for every-thing."

# CHAPTER 6
## Love Bearing

"Behold the Lamb of God which beareth the sin of the world" (John 1:29).

"God can have no delight or union with an creature, but because his well-beloved Son, the express image of his person, is found in it. Holy love became incarnate in the creature."

"Love is not holy love until it becomes universal, that is to say, not love for some only, but love for all." (William Law)

The second letter in the alphabet of love is bearing, which in actual fact is the meaning of forgiveness. How our Lord emphasized this second letter or principle in the kingdom of love. If the mind of Christ is to be in us, there must be this willingness to bear all that life and other people put upon us, just as Christ did. "Behold the Lamb of God which beareth the sin of the world."

To bear means to accept any and all wrong that others do to us, any burden they may put upon us, any infringements of our rights, any losses they may cause us. It goes even further than accepting with joy, because it is the very essence of forgiveness. To forgive is to bear in this way anything that another may do to us, and to say as Christ did, "I choose to bear all that you do to me and still love you and long for your salvation, your rescue and release from sin and self. I will bear whatever it may cost me, and I mean to use the creative power of forgiveness to help you all I can."

Moreover, to forgive is not just to remit a penalty, but to bear the cost of the sin oneself, yes, and even more than that, as far as possible to atone, namely, to undo the consequences of the sin committed by another.

When a father's love leads him to forgive a prodigal son, he must undertake to pay off as far as possible all that son's debts. For he must not allow any innocent or wronged person to suffer as a result of the wrongdoing of this one whom he loves and is ready to forgive. Anything else would be forgiveness at the expense of someone else, and would not be real forgiveness at all. For it is really true that we cannot actually forgive any wrongdoing except that which is done against ourself.

Only the wronged person has the right and privilege to forgive, that is why only God can forgive all sin. Therefore the father of the erring son may forgive the shame and dishonor done to his name, and the anguish caused to his own heart, and he may, as far as is possible, atone for the son's wrongdoing by seeking to undo its effects on others, but the actual sin against another he cannot forgive. That is why a just judge must condemn and punish all offenders. To forgive them would be an injustice. The only offenses he may justly forgive and not bring to the judgment bar at all are the wrongs which have been done to him personally.

Love always seeks not only to forgive, but wherever possible to atone. As humans we can often do very little to atone for the sins of those we love. We can bear whatever loss or cost their wrongdoing involves us in, and make atonement or restitution where possible to the wronged ones. But no one, for instance, can atone to a bereaved family for the murder of a loved one; still less for innocence deliberately destroyed in a child. Nor, however much we may long to do so, may we remit the just punishment he must undergo. That is why a parent must punish a child, that he may learn not to wrong or harm others, and to discipline his nature and learn self-control.

There are many, many losses which only God can make good. But through our Lord Jesus Christ the world, yes, the whole world, does receive atonement. There is no wrong done to ourselves or to anybody else in the whole wide world which God himself will not atone for, namely, undo the consequences. He has pledged himself to this. That is the greatest of all reasons why we must forgive others, because there is no wrong which we suffer at the hands of others but that we shall receive atonement for it fully. That is to say, no evil which is done to us can harm us ultimately, for it will be compensated for by God himself. Therefore if God is going to atone for it, there is in one sense nothing for us to forgive, and to harbor an unforgiving spirit is absurd, to say the least of it. When faith accepts this glorious fact, it is obvious that forgiveness becomes a primary duty, a joy, and a privilege.

The habit of glad forgiveness, through willingness to bear the wrong and to atone as far as possible, is an inescapable and glorious law in the kingdom of love. And it is one of the principles which we are slowest to learn, perhaps because we so often tell ourselves that to forgive may leave the wrongdoer impenitent and unchanged, and ourselves unable to help them to realize their sin.

Never! That fear is a lie, though I believed

it for a long time, and have heard it from the lips of many earnest Christians. "Never forgive until the wrongdoer is penitent" is the doctrine of the Pharisees. It results in many an earnest Christian becoming colder and colder, harder and harder, and more and more unloving, because they have made themselves sincerely believe that the other person is wholly in the wrong and they themselves are blameless. Therefore the other person must take the first step towards reconciliation, by confessing their fault and asking for forgiveness.

The truth is that we cannot change anyone, or help them to penitence, or cause them to hate the sin, until we have fully forgiven all there is to forgive, and undertake to bear the wrong. The only thing needed on the other side is a willingness to accept the forgiveness and that is their responsibility.

For forgiveness is a gloriously creative principle, and can generate in us (as it did, of course, in a unique way in our Lord) a saving and liberating power which can reach and change others. In its very essence, forgiveness involves creative love thinking (which is the subject of the next chapter), and only creative love thinking is supremely powerful. What a vast amount of our spiritual impotency and powerlessness to rescue others, and to bring them into touch with Christ, is due to our failure to understand and practice this principle.

Before Peter asked the Lord his question

as to how often he should forgive his brother, the Lord had spoken these significant words in connection with trespasses committed by a brother.

"Whatsoever ye shall bind on earth, shall be bound in heaven (i.e., remain unfreed) and whatsoever ye shall loose on earth, shall be loosed (go free) in heaven" (Matt. 18:18). The great loosing and freeing power is the power generated by forgiveness.

Of course, in ourselves, and by our own power, we are utterly unable to bring ourselves to forgive even the smallest sins, or to bear even the slightest infringements of our rights, if the wrongdoer is someone we dislike, or a real enemy. But it is easy to forgive those we love. Indeed, the more we love, the more eagerly we hasten to forgive and to bear gladly, and to find some way to atone. Of course, because it is the nature of love to forgive; and it is the nature of dislike, indifference and hate to be unable to forgive.

Of course this principle does not contradict the need for repentance, punishment and justice. These also are vital principles, and, as we have seen already, we have no right to forgive and remit the penalty against sins committed against other people, only those committed against ourselves. But repentance, punishment and justice, in actual fact, do not belong to forgiveness at all, but to the great law of righteousness.

Forgiveness is essentially substitutionary,

94

a willingness to bear oneself all the consequences of a sin committed against us by another person, namely, instead of the sinner suffering for what he has done to us, we suffer ourselves. A judge must condemn a man for having made others suffer. But he does not call that forgiving the man, he calls it justice. A parent must punish a rebellious child who causes harm to others, but a mother never calls punishment forgiveness, neither can she justly say, after the punishment is over, that she is now able or ready to forgive, because the child has already suffered retribution or punishment for the offense.

Love is never free to remit the penalty of an offense done to someone else, but is always gloriously free to forgive and remit the penalty of an offense against oneself. This is the principle of bearing, of forgiveness. It is the principle our Lord always practiced, and which he taught his followers to practice.

What if it seems that we really cannot bring ourselves to forgive? What if, in spite of all our efforts and prayers and struggles, we find the wrong done to us to be something we believe we never can forget or get free from? I can never cease to be grateful beyond all words to one who was almost a stranger to me, who yet put into my hands the clue or the key to forgiveness when it feels impossible to forgive.

There was a time when I found myself in just that position. I felt I had been treated so badly, and obliged to go through such un-deserved suffering, that, try as I would, I could not forgive. I truly wanted to forgive. I knew that as a Christian I must forgive, but I just could not do it. I used to ask other Christians to help me to do so, to show me the way to do so, and though they were all very sympathetic when they heard what I had been through, none of them seemed able to give me the clue I so much needed as to how to forgive and forget.

Over and over again all the circumstances and details kept intruding into my mind, and with the memory came all the feelings of bitterness and self pity. When I tried to meet the Lord in my quiet times, exactly the same thing happened, I could think of nothing else, and the more I thought of it, the worse I felt, and the more impossible it seemed to be able to forget.

Undoubtedly resentment and bitterness and unforgiveness not only poison the thought life, but they can play havoc with the body as well, for they are deadly destructive things. Whether they were the whole cause, or only weakened my bodily defenses against infection, at any rate after a time I became really ill, and one day, while I was in bed, feeling very wretched indeed, a stranger walked into my room, saying that she had heard from mutual friends that I was ill, and that she had felt led to come and see me.

And as we talked together, somehow it all came out again, and I found myself telling her the old familiar story with all its bitter details. And at the end I added despairingly, "The awful part is that I can't forgive and forget. I just long to do so, because it comes in between the Lord and me the whole time, but I can't."

She said, "I will tell you the secret of how to forgive and forget. As long as you talk about this thing and discuss it with others, just so long will you never get free from it. But if you will take this wrong done to you to the cross of our Lord, and confess it to him exactly as though it was a wrong done against himself, and ask him to forgive it completely and to forget it, just as you ask him to forgive and forget your own sins against him, and if you will leave it there at the cross and promise him never to touch it again, namely, that you will never speak of it to anyone else, but act as though the wrong had never been committed at all, and if you refuse to listen to anyone who mentions it, you will go free and forget it altogether."

Take it to the cross, and leave it there, and promise never to touch it again. That is the secret. I found it worked absolutely perfectly and at once. I asked the Lord to forgive the thing which I thought had wronged me, and I promised that I would never let the subject cross my lips again. From that day to this I have never mentioned it to anybody. When at first people tried to sympathize or to ask about it, I simply said, "Please excuse me, but I have promised the Lord never to refer to it." From the first occasion that I made that answer, all desire to speak of it went from me.

The thing, of course had been done to me and I still had to bear the difficult consequences, but they no longer had power to trouble me. And strangely enough, something else happened. The memory of it did not entirely go because, as I say, the consequences remained and had to be borne. But the memory of all the bitter painful details went completely, and all that remained was the real, true good and blessing, which I now discovered the experience had brought to me. It was soon like a prickly thorn bush, which had suddenly burst into radiant, golden bloom, and all the thorns were hidden and forgotten by the mass of glory bursting forth from them.

"We went through fire and through water, but thou, Lord, broughtest us forth into a wealthy place" (Ps. 66:12). This is the experience of every soul who has learned the royal prerogative of love, to forgive and to bear.

There is also another glorious thing connected with bearing, which I hardly like to mention because in my own life it has been so rare, and it is perhaps the most holy experience which can come to us. Others have much more right to speak of it than I. And yet among all my Christian acquaintances, no one had led me to suppose that bearing could have such a holy and unique joy connected with it, and that perhaps this, in a special way, is what the apostle Paul referred to when he wrote of the fellowship of his sufferings. There are two words which perhaps we only really understand in brief, infrequent flashes, like a sudden rending of a veil and a glimpse into heaven itself. They are the words identification and vicarious.

Once I was with someone who seemed to be stumbling and hurting others, without in the least realizing it, and apparently quite unwilling to be shown the fact. One day a most overwhelmingly humiliating experience befell that person. I was present at the time, and I remember as if it were yesterday sitting beside that one, inwardly writhing with agony of pain I had never believed possible, all the almost unbearable exasperation I had often felt, swallowed up by the suffering.

At last, when it was over, and it had seemed to be endless, I felt that I could not let that one go away alone, with a sense of awful loneliness and that everyone was against her. I slipped my arm through hers and walked with her, feeling suddenly as though all the unfriendly eyes were robbed of their power to hurt, because there were two of us bearing it together.

After a while I at last found power to break the silence, and I said, "Did it seem too dreadful? You know I was bearing it with you. I hoped you would feel that." And then an affectionate, appreciative answer was made, which made me realize with almost stunned surprise that no suffering had been felt at all, so strong had been the belief that everyone else was completely wrong in their condemnation, that there had been no point in paying attention to them.

As this realization broke over me, I experienced suddenly the deepest, richest thrill of joy that I have ever known—and how much joy has come my way, but none like this. The understanding came to me with an ecstasy of thankfulness and delight, that in some way all the pain and humiliation had been borne by me, not by the other one, that we had changed places, and all had fallen upon me instead.

For the first time in my life I understood how glad, how unutterably glad the Lord must have been to bear all the worst of the shame and agony and loneliness of sin, for us. "Vicarious" suddenly became the most lovely word I had ever heard. Lovers and parents, I suppose, must be the people who know most about this glory of bearing instead of the loved one. But it is unutterably blessed that the Lord is willing to allow the least of his disciples to know something about it also, if they will only be willing to learn the ABC's of love.

When I tried haltingly a little later on to share this experience with someone else concerned, I was astonished that their instant reaction was, "But that is utterly immoral. They ought to have felt it all themselves."

All I could answer was, "I don't understand about that. All I knew was that I was thinking and feeling for a moment as God thinks and feels."

Just there perhaps, yes, just there, love's power to save and rescue and help others is at its greatest. Can any prayer that one can utter on a cross go unanswered? Think of what happened when the King of Love, hanging on a cross between two thieves, praying for those who crucified him, said, "Father, forgive them—they know not what they do." His was the right to forgive and to save the whole world.

Sometimes we are so slow to learn and practice these things, and perhaps even remain blind to the fact that as Christians we must learn them, that perhaps people looking on may be tempted to feel that we are not Christians after all, in spite of all our profession. But it is comforting to know that the very fact that gradually, stage by stage, we have come to realize these truths more fully, is in itself the guarantee that we have been in the way all the time, and the Lord has been developing us gradually, as we were able to bear it.

This fact also should make us very slow to judge one another, because we vary so greatly in the speed with which we develop understanding of spiritual things, neither do we learn the different aspects of truth in the same order. Just as plants vary in the speed of their growth, so often it depends greatly on environment and temperament how soon we shall be able to receive new truth. It is really pitiable how often we condemn someone for heresy, simply because they have grasped a phase of truth which we are still too immature to understand, but which we shall have to learn too, later on.

Once again, as with the principle of accepting with joy, so with the principle of bearing, it may be easier to forgive big sins, just because it is easier to see that we ought to do so, than to forgive the little irritating defects and blemishes in others we may live and work with. We tell ourselves that they ought to be willing to change those exasperating ways and habits, and that it is incumbent on us to help them to realize this, nay rather that it is our obvious duty to do so, for if they don't realize their faults by being told about them, they will feel no incentive to correct them.

How greatly life is harassed and marred by this passion so many of us display, of trying to alter people and make them what we think they ought to be; all the more so if they happen to be fellow Christians, and have therefore less right than the unsaved to be aggravating and obstructive! How greatly lessened, indeed sometimes altogether removed, is the wear and tear and nerve strain when we give up trying to alter people and concentrate on learning to adapt ourselves to them, realizing that ours is the privilege and joy of bearing the little minor frets, as well as the big wrongs, because this is the nature of love.

Evelyn Underhill, in one of her letters to a devoted Christian whose nerves, however, were fretted almost unbearably by the slowness and fussiness of a fellow worker, wrote most delightfully and pertinently in this way: "Why should you object to her fussing over everything she does and worrying all the time, any more than you should expect her to object to your passion for reading and burying yourself in a book when she thinks you ought to be helping in her fussy arrangements?"

We must face the fact that temperamental differences are the real cause of much which we think we must alter, simply because it jars on us; and the secret of escaping frayed nerves and irritable tempers is to accept and bear these things, and the extra work which they involve us in, as being part of the glorious adventure and discipline of being made like our Lord.

There is no doubt about it, that this is the greatest of all problems on the mission field. What real agonies of nervous irritability slow and quick people can go through when they have to work together in the isolation of a mission station; or tidy and critical people who have to work with untidy, easy going, but nicer tempered people; and the very conscientious and exact people, who find themselves in harness with very quick, and slapdash, but perhaps much more brilliant partners.

The fact that by temperament there are things which seem terribly important to some people, and absurdly unimportant to others, should expose the futility of trying to alter one another to suit our own pattern. Why try to change? Why not joyfully accept the principle of bearing, and get all the stimulation and delightful excitement out of overcoming our own intense desire to reform the other person and learn to adjust our own irritating temper to the situation.

Of course, as far as teachers and parents are concerned, children must be trained, and so must young adults preparing for special work and service. But why constitute oneself a solo training school for others on the mission field! Or, for that matter, in the home or anywhere else? It only means we wear ourselves to pieces and miss all the blessing of bearing, and so receiving the power to help them in quite a different way.

But what if our fellow workers seem to be causing others to stumble? When our Lord told his disciples to wash one another's feet, did he actually mean that we should faithfully help them to see their faults and point out to them where they offend? I don't think so. Indeed, I think that is just the method the disciples were practicing in the upper room, trying to make somebody else see that they ought to be performing the lowly task of feet washing, or at least to be ready to take their share in it.

I think our Lord definitely taught elsewhere that that idea is like trying to take a mote out of your brother's eye when you have a beam in your own. What he taught on this occasion in the upper room was simply this: that bearing and forgiving one another, and finding delight (not martyrdom) in serving one another, is the surest and most powerful way of being able to help them, without, as in this case, saying a word to any of the offenders.

Surely to wash one another's feet is to cleanse them completely in our thoughts, and to find through the lowly but adventurous service of love a means of helping them. If we cleanse them in our thoughts, that means, of course, that we cannot possibly brood on their aggravating ways, but can only laugh (as rudely as possible) at ourselves and say, "What an idiot I am. He or she is made like that, or has grown like that, and I can't do anything about altering it, except through creative prayer thinking. So I will concentrate on that, and hope and pray that they will deal with my own exasperating or stumbling habits in the same way."

I know of two people who I am pretty certain have treated me in this way, without saying a single word. And I wonder, oh so thankfully, just how often they needed to wash my feet in this way in their prayers, until I came to understand some of the things I shall be writing about in the next chapter.

The wonder and joy of it is, that as we learn and practice using the alphabet of love, the whole of life becomes transfigured, and where love reigns, the very joy of heaven itself is felt.

# CHAPTER 7

# Creative Love Thinking

"Be not overcome of evil, but overcome evil with good" (Rom. 12:21).

Love thinks only lovely thoughts. It is happy to love.

The principles of accepting with joy, and of bearing, were principles which I had known about and wanted to practice most of my Christian life, though it was very slowly and painfully that I learned the lessons which I have been trying to share in the last two chapters. However, what I had completely failed to realize and understand is the tremendous power liberated by creative love thinking.

All the time I had been trying to pump and pump up power through earnest prayer, earnest surrender, and earnest devotion to the Lord. But now I found that when the reign of love begins in the mind, power of an absolutely new kind is continually generated and liberated, as though the Niagara Falls of love, emptying themselves into the whole love-controlled personality, fall as it were on the turbines in the power station of the mind and produce a volume of power which one never dreamed of before, and which the Holy Spirit uses and directs as he chooses. The old rusty pump of earnest effort is swept away in the flood and needed no more. When I first began to experience this new power at work in my mind, the only name by which I could describe it was creative love thinking.

Naturally this influx of new power becomes greater as we learn to yield more and more to the control of love, and to block every avenue to the waiting floods of destructive thinking. It was particularly in my own prayer life that I began to discover what a complete transformation this new principle of thinking only creative thoughts could produce. I discovered that love can only think lovely thoughts. That our Beloved "feedeth amongst the lilies," and that Paul was right indeed when he said, "Whatsoever things are true . . . honest . . . just . . . pure . . . lovely . . . and of good report" (Phil. 4:8), these and these things alone are what we are to think about and to pray about.

All my Christian life I had been worried and distressed because I found that prayer meetings so often seemed to me to be dreadfully dreary and unreal, to such an extent, in fact, that they were a real discipline, and one I was always trying to evade, without appearing to be too dreadfully unspiritual and lacking in keenness. I heard many earnest people express the opinion that the weekly prayer meeting indicated the spiritual temperature of a church, and that you could estimate a Christian's keenness by his regular attendance at the prayer meeting— or absence from it. This made me feel most uncomfortable and guilty, for if I was to be judged by the enthusiasm with which I attended most prayer meetings, I was tepid indeed.

Chiefly I think it was because I felt that we did such a tremendous lot of talking to God at great length, without an interval for listening to him. And that sometimes we addressed our Lord in a way we would never dream or even dare to do if we could actually see him standing before us. In fact our prayers were sometimes like a long monologue, elaborating a list of things he already knew, explaining in great detail, as though otherwise he might not understand all the facts, and reminding him, in case he might forget some of them, of needs all round the world, and perhaps, quite unconsciously, proffering him a little advice as to what to do about them. Instead of giving him time to speak to us and show us just what it was he wanted us to join him in praying about.

On the other hand I very greatly enjoyed small, informal prayer times with close friends, when we could pray together about our needs and seek for guidance—and intercede quite freely for others, in a way which of course, was never possible in a public prayer meeting, as any mention of personalities would be carried on the wings of the air to the ears of the people who had been thus prayed for.

It was just here that I was so painfully blind. I did not realize that in fact, under the guise of prayer for others, instead of building them up, all too often I was tearing them to pieces, exposing before those who were praying with me the frailties, weaknesses and sins (real or imagined) of those I was supposed to be praying for, and at the same time impressing more and more deeply upon my own consciousness and awareness the very things which I was asking they might be freed from.

So that instead of being helped by such prayer times to be more patient and loving toward them, the next time I met them I was sure to be more irritated by, and less able to be patient and loving with the person I had been so earnestly praying for. I have discovered that it is a fact that one can almost always tell when someone has been praying in this way, because the prayer always backfires, as it were, and cripples their manner toward us.

By the tender mercy of our dear Lord I was at last cured, once and for all, of this habit of destructive thinking towards others under the guise of prayer. It was not a pleasant way to have my eyes opened, but if only I had been able to learn it much sooner!

It was during a time of very special inward and outward strain and stress, when I was finding it very difficult to accept certain details in the situation. I had met with a friend on purpose that we might pray together ostensibly that I might be given victory in these difficult circumstances, but in fact that I might ease myself by expressing all the bitter exasperation that I was feeling towards some of my fellow workers. Under the guise of asking to be delivered myself, and claiming the assurance that when two of you shall agree as touching anything, it shall be given you, I began unmasking all the faults in others which I was feeling so bitter about, and praying for deliverance and victory.

On that occasion the prayer was answered —I might almost say dramatically answered, and my whole habit of prayer transformed from that afternoon onward, with most remarkable thoroughness!

It happened to be a very hot day, and believing everybody else to be absent from the house, we left the door of my room ajar. It seems that someone whom I had always considered extremely unspiritually minded, because he was not attracted to these intimate little prayer meetings, emerging from the room beneath us, found that the prayer going on in my room was distinctly audible on the landing below.

Concluding (as I now feel with absolute rightness) that no petitions would be uttered to the Lord which would be of an unedifying nature for others to hear, he lingered on the landing. With the result that word quickly went round that the holy little prayer meetings carried on in my apartment were in reality nothing but a gossip club, in which everybody's faults and failings were pitilessly exposed under the guise of praying for them.

Never, I feel, can I repay the debt of gratitude which I owe to that person! From the moment that I was made aware of what had happened, as I said before, with absolutely dramatic suddenness, the veil was torn away from my mind, the hypocrisy was exposed, and I saw the truth. Standing absolutely abject with shame before the Lord, I vowed to him that I would never either silently or audibly pray anything about anyone else which I would not pray if I knew that they were able to hear me or to read my thoughts. At the moment I stumbled, decidedly bruised, and almost blinded by the light, into the realm of creative love thinking, which I believe to be the essence of true intercession.

Over and over again, when I try to tell people about this experience and the vow, they exclaim, "But you can't shut your eyes to the wrong things in the lives of other people and say that they are right. If you want to help a person, you can't do it if you blind yourself to their faults, and surely you must pray for them to be rescued from those sins?"

No, creative love thinking certainly does not mean refusing to recognize sin, or pretending it does not matter, or that it is not our business to try and help; but it means a completely transformed reaction to sin, and to any faults and blemishes which may appear in others. When seen quite plainly with no slurring over, they simply present us with a challenge to see exactly the opposite, namely, to imagine what a person would be like if completely delivered, radiant, loving, happy, praising, perfect in grace and with the beauty of the Lord shining upon them; and to join with the Lord in claiming the beginning and the continuation of that transformation, at the same time shutting out completely the picture of the actual, present condition of that person.

Surely that is what our Lord's own prayers are, creative thinking about each one of us; seeing us with all our besetting sins, weaknesses, ugly blemishes completely removed, and the whole personality as it will be when his perfect work in us is finished. What a blessed use for the imagination! And oh for how many years, as I now realized, had I prostituted my imagination and used it for just the opposite kind of destructive imagining.

Perhaps an illustration will help. When I first went to Palestine I lived in Haifa, a big port city at the foot of Mount Carmel. As caretaker of the mission property in the middle of the city we had an Arab, very small in stature, who had a real passion for gardening. In any little heap of soil which he could collect together he planted seeds, and they always grew in the most astonishing way, no matter where he put them. One day he came to me very impressively and said, "Come and look at my violets, Miss Hurnard, they are simply magnificent."

"Why, Khalil," I exclaimed, "surely you can't have got violets to bloom so early in the season?" He led me then to a little patch of what looked like completely bare earth, and kneeling down, pointed with his finger, and wherever he pointed I saw, as I leaned closer, a minute green shoot.

"They are all coming up," he said exultantly. "I rather wondered if they would, as this is not a very congenial situation for them. But we shall have a grand lot of blooms later."

And so we did. But with the eye of love and faith he saw, even at that stage of immaturity, while there was still no indication at all of the purple, perfumed petals that we associate with violets, the lovely vision of what eventually would be. He watered and weeded and zealously fenced off the little patch of earth, so that careless passersby would not tread upon it, until the seedlings blossomed fully into what he so happily, albeit so patiently, waited for. That seems to me a lovely illustration of real creative love intercession, seeing with the eye of faith the lovely future, and cooperating with the Lord of Love in making it come to pass.

So now I seek always to pray only such prayers as I would like those I prayed for to hear, and to think such lovely radiant thoughts about what they were being changed into that whenever they knew I was praying with someone else they would want to come tiptoeing up to the door, to try to gain a vision of the lovely, radiant destiny awaiting them.

But to harp on faults in our prayers, to visualize them and then to pray for their removal can, as I have already suggested, be very destructive. It is like trampling down the very thing which we want to encourage. How much better to behold the desired perfection, and to concentrate on that, and leave the Lord, as a skilled gardener, to prune and remove the blemishes as and when he sees fit. I have often wondered whose loving, creative thinking about me— seeing me fully delivered from the habit of destructive praying—cooperated with the Lord, and the Lord, smiling gently to himself, allowed that friend to loiter on the landing below my bedroom door.

After that experience I must confess that it became harder than ever to enjoy the ordinary kind of prayer meeting, where we seemed to spend the whole time uttering audible petitions in turn, with no time left for seeing the perfect pattern that the Lord wanted. Would it not be better, perhaps to spend at least half the time in a prayer meeting in corporate silence, to get together thinking creative love thoughts and getting a vision of the perfect goal we are supposed to be praying for? I suppose, however, that always, and quite rightly, as temperaments differ so greatly, different sorts of prayer meetings will continue to help different sorts of people!

Sometime later I came across a book by Agnes Sanford, called *The Healing Light*. And this greatly enriched and clarified my new ideas about creative love thinking. She emphasizes this different kind of prayer so clearly, especially in connection with prayer for bodily healing.

One instance mentioned in the book impressed me very greatly. On one occasion a group of women had been asked to pray for a sick person far away in a distant city. It so happened that all four of them were at that time suffering from various aches and pains themselves, and could not help being very conscious of their own bodily symptoms, so that apparently none of them in their prayer time had been able to see or picture the sick person absolutely perfect in health and freed from all pain. And the following day the leader of the prayer group received a cable from the distant city which said, "Check up on what you are doing. The patient seems worse!"

Is it not possible, knowing the tremendous power of thought as we are coming to realize, that when we think destructive or critical thoughts about others we do in some way project those thoughts until they may touch the thoughts of others destructively? It is worth pondering over this possibility, especially in connection with our prayer life. For it may be that we may gloriously touch and influence the thoughts of others when we think about them with creative love. And when we think disparagingly or despisingly or unlovingly about them, we may be touching their minds in a poisonous way. What a responsibility this suggests. Ought we not to heed this warning at every prayer meeting? Check up on what you are doing! The world, or the church's condition, seems worse!

# CHAPTER 8
# Unity
# of
# Love

"There came a voice out of the cloud saying, 'This is my beloved Son, hear him.' And when the voice was past, Jesus was found alone" (Luke 9:35, 36).

"I beseech you that ye walk worthy of the vocation . . . endeavouring to keep the unity of the Spirit in the bond of peace . . . with all lowliness and meekness, with longsuffering, forebearing one another in love" (Eph. 4:1-3).

And now to go back to the great question at the beginning of this book. What is the real unity of the Body of Christ? How are we to foster and practice it? What is to be our attitude towards those Christians we cannot conscientiously agree with and who, we fear, will lead others into error?

How far ought we to join in cooperation with other Christian groups who do not use our form of worship, or whose methods are different from our own? How should we speak about these differences in teaching and in interpretation to non-Christians? Above all, how should we warn others of danger and engage in combat against real error and denial of our Lord, without doing despite to the Holy Spirit of Love, and damaging ourselves by using destructive thinking? For if destructive habits of thought can work such havoc in the Church of Christ as history records down through the ages, so that even now in this twentieth century we continue to split up and divide into more and more factions and groups all the time, what is the practical healing and uniting principle which we are to practice?

"Ye have left your first love," was the message of the Lord to the first church which began to split and divide up on this very subject of "trying them that say they are prophets, and are not, but are liars" (Rev. 2:2). It seems then the primary cause of disunity is to be found in this, i.e., leaving our first love, not necessarily growing cold and lacking in fervor, but transferring our chief or supreme love to another object, away from Christ himself. Transferring perhaps, our loyalty and warmest love and interest away from the person of Christ to the Church herself? Or our particular section of the Church? Or to sound doctrine, or the faith once delivered to us by the saints?

And in all those cases we immediately find ourselves with a transferred center of combat also, and we shall be versus everybody else who isn't centering on the same object, and like Saul and other really sincere and devout Pharisees, all unknowingly we may even find that we have been fighting against Christ himself.

If the real cause of disunity and weakness in the Church is through having left the first center of love and loyalty, namely, our Lord himself, who is Savior and King and Leader, then the cure for each one of us individually, and corporately, will be to get back to the center we have left. We must get back to our first love and center, the Lord of the Church himself, for even the Church and the doctrines and the gospel itself, take second place to him. And then learn from him to love all our fellow members of his body as he loves them and to behave towards them as he behaves towards us.

For he said, "I have given you an example, that ye should do as I have done to you" (John 13:15). We find over and over again that he continues to give the very blessing, yes, a power to help others to follow him, to many people whom we feel ought not to enjoy those blessings or to have that power, because of their unsound teaching.

If we will but practice the ABC's of love we shall, each one individually, find the way to loving unity, without uniformity, with all others who are practicing the same principles of the kingdom of love.

1. Love accepts and loves all who truly love the Lord Jesus and make him central in their hearts. This attitude puts us into the relationship of children in one large family, diverse in temperament, interest, abilities and gifts, work and pastimes, but all deeply interested in each other and lovingly ready to help whenever need arises or opportunity occurs, and never, by any chance, decrying a member of the family to outsiders. Love accepts with joy. That is the first lovely principle in the kingdom of love.

There is an interesting account of one of God's servants listening at a theological college to a professor who was discrediting the Virgin Birth in one of his lectures, and yet the professor himself was a sincere and earnest follower of the Lord Jesus, though intellectually he could not accept that particular doctrine. As he listened, this servant of God grew more and more troubled and wretched until he could bear it no longer, and, lifting his heart to the Lord, he exclaimed inwardly, "Lord, what is the truth? What am I to believe? And how can one who professes to love and serve you deny the Virgin Birth?"

And gently and clearly, it seemed to him, the Lord gave an answer, which for him was the perfect answer. He said, "I was born of a virgin, but I accept those who don't see it."

Some glad day we shall all see and understand a great deal of truth to which we are now quite blind, and then we shall be very thankful indeed that the Lord did not wait, nor refuse to accept us, until we could and would understand all that he meant us to know about him. It was a long time after he began to follow the Lord that Peter came to understand that he was actually the Son of God as well as beloved Leader and Master.

2. Then love bears all that irks and burdens and disappoints us in those we are put to work with and with whom we find we disagree.

3. And love learns to pray for all such creatively, so that transforming power is liberated in their lives.

If we, as individuals and churches, practice these three principles, and allow love to reign in our hearts and minds, we shall find that our attitude and behavior towards others will be all the time creative of unity and not of distrust and separation. We shall undoubtedly differ in our individual decisions as to how far the Holy Spirit of love means us to go in outward cooperation, but we cannot go wrong in loving. Only love is not in word, but in deed. It does not mean saying with our lips that we do love all the true members of Christ's body, and yet acting as though we heartily disapprove of them and warning others against them. Love must express itself, and seeks for every opportunity to do so.

What sort of unity will be the outcome of creative love thinking and acting? Not an artificial uniformity, but the unity and power which belongs to every individual who practices with other individuals and groups, creative love thinking towards one another, and supreme devotion to our Lord Jesus Christ. Then he will use our witness just as he chooses, and manifest himself to the world through us.

When we have entered into that unity we shall be able to rejoice in quite a new way in the glorious truth that God uses a multitude of other ways and means to help those who have not been able to find help through the things which have been so indescribably helpful to us personally. We shall exult exceedingly over the great multitude which no man can number who have been brought to Christ by others, and in ways which we ourselves could not have followed, and perhaps even though, or in spite of, teaching which we thought was quite erroneous.

> In essentials, unity.
> In nonessentials, liberty.
> In all things, charity.

And perhaps all the great essentials can be summed up in the words spoken by the voice of God from heaven, "This is my beloved Son in whom I am well pleased. Hear him."